The Mystery in Tornado Alley

"Get to a ditch!" Nancy shouted. "Curl up and cover your heads!"

Nancy was glad now that Hannah had brought along the book about Oklahoma on their trip. She read what people should do if they were caught on the highway during a tornado.

When the RV stopped, Nancy opened the side doors and everyone rushed out into the blinding rain.

Above the noise of the rain Nancy heard another noise. It sounded like the roar of a thousand jet planes.

That's it, she thought. That's what tornadoes are supposed to sound like.

All of a sudden the rain slackened but not the noise, and the sky filled with flying debris.

As she buried her face in the wet grass, Nancy wondered if they'd get out of this alive.

Nancy Drew
Mystery Stories

Available from MINSTREL Books

NANCY DREW® 155

THE MYSTERY IN TORNADO ALLEY

CAROLYN KEENE

A MINSTREL® BOOK

Published by POCKET BOOKS
New York   London   Toronto   Sydney   Singapore

This book is a work of fiction. Names, characters, places and incidents
are products of the author's imagination or are used fictitiously. Any
resemblance to actual events or locales or persons living or dead is
entirely coincidental.

A MINSTREL PAPERBACK *Original*

A Minstrel Book published by
POCKET BOOKS, a division of Simon & Schuster Inc.
1230 Avenue of the Americas, New York, NY 10020

Copyright © 2000 by Simon & Schuster Inc.

ISBN: 0-671-04264-5

First Minstrel Books printing July 2000

10 9 8 7 6 5 4 3 2 1

NANCY DREW, NANCY DREW MYSTERY STORIES,
A MINSTREL BOOK and colophon are registered
trademarks of Simon & Schuster Inc.

Cover art by Ernie Norcia

Printed in the U.S.A.

Contents

THE MYSTERY
IN TORNADO ALLEY

1

Terror from the Sky

Nancy Drew paced back and forth across the living room. "What could be keeping Dad and Hannah?" she muttered. "They were only going to the pharmacy to fill one of Hannah's prescriptions." She glanced at her watch. "We'll miss our plane if they're not back soon."

Suddenly Nancy heard what sounded like a bus pull into the Drews' driveway. She rushed to the front window and looked out.

"Oh, wow!" she cried.

Nancy let the curtain drop and raced out the front door of her house, her reddish blond hair flying.

"What's with the RV, Dad?" she called as Carson

1

Drew and their housekeeper, Hannah Gruen, stepped down from the huge motor home.

"This is what we're driving to Oklahoma," Mr. Drew replied.

Nancy blinked her bright blue eyes in surprise. "I thought we were going to fly."

Hannah shook her head. "It's all my fault, Nancy. I decided I might want to bring back some things from Cousin Bertha's house, so your father kindly agreed to rent this RV and return the airline tickets."

"We should have plenty of room now for anything Hannah wants to bring back," Mr. Drew said. He paused. "Is something wrong, Nancy?"

Nancy sighed. "Oh, no, Dad, not really. It's just that . . . well, you know how much I love to fly."

"That I do, Nancy," her father said. "That I do."

"How long will it take us to get to Oklahoma?" Nancy ventured.

"A couple of days," her father replied, grinning. "Are you worried about getting bored without a mystery to solve?"

Nancy returned his grin. "Oh, I'll find *something* to keep myself occupied."

Nancy knew how important this trip was to Hannah. Their housekeeper had unexpectedly received a letter from a lawyer in Medicine Bluff, Oklahoma, informing her that she had inherited a farm from her cousin Bertha, whom she hadn't heard from in years. Because Carson Drew was not only her employer of many years but also the most prominent lawyer in River Heights, Hannah asked him for advice. After Hannah decided that she didn't want to give up her life in River Heights and move, Mr. Drew advised her to sell the property. Hannah wanted to see it first, though, because she and Bertha had been close as children, so it was decided to go to Medicine Bluff to take care of the legal matters in person.

Just then Nancy's two best friends, Bess Marvin and George Fayne, stepped out of the back of the RV. "Surprise!" they cried.

"What's going on here?" Nancy asked.

Mr. Drew laughed. "Hannah knew you'd be disappointed about not flying, so she asked Bess and George if they could go with us. They can. It'll be like a party."

"All right!" Nancy cheered.

Bess and George rushed up to hug her. The two girls were cousins, but they were physical opposites. George was tall, slim, and very athletic. She had dark hair and eyes. Bess was shorter and had a fuller figure. Her blond hair was the color of straw, and she had pale blue eyes.

"Get your things, Nancy," Mr. Drew said. "The rest of us are ready to go."

Nancy, Bess, and George ran into the house to help Nancy retrieve her luggage, then they all got back into the RV.

"This thing is huge," Nancy said.

"It's like a house on wheels," Hannah said.

When everyone was seated and buckled in, Mr. Drew backed out of the driveway.

"We'll make St. Louis tonight," Mr. Drew said. "Then tomorrow we'll be in Medicine Bluff, Oklahoma."

"I'm really looking forward to the trip, Nancy," George said. "We've all been so busy lately, we haven't had any really good long talks."

"I met the cutest guy last week," Bess said. "He used to live in Oklahoma. Right before his family moved to River Heights, their house was blown away by a tornado. He said they were lucky to be alive."

"That's terrible," Nancy said. "You hear a lot about tornadoes in that part of the country."

"Well, I certainly hope we're not in one while we're there," Bess said.

"Me, too. They're so powerful," Nancy said. "I saw a documentary about them on television."

Hannah shivered.

"What's wrong?" Nancy asked.

"I wish you girls wouldn't talk about tornadoes," Hannah replied. She reached into a bag by her feet. "I bought this book about Oklahoma right after I heard about the farm. It has pictures of tornadoes in it."

Nancy took the book from Hannah.

"Oh, Bess, George! Look at this," she said. "It

4

shows the tornado that hit Oklahoma City. Look how huge it is!"

"It makes you wonder what must have been going through people's minds when they saw that tornado coming," Bess said. "I would have been terrified."

"People were," Nancy said. "It was an F5."

"What does that mean?" Hannah asked.

"F stands for Fujita. He was the scientist who came up with the damage ranking for tornadoes," Nancy replied. "F0 tornadoes are the weakest. They have winds of only forty to seventy-two miles per hour."

"That's still a lot of wind," Mr. Drew said. "It's almost hurricane strength."

"You're right, Dad, but F5 tornadoes have winds of over 261 miles per hour," Nancy said. "They're the most powerful storms on earth."

"I'm glad we don't have tornadoes in River Heights," George said.

"Actually, River Heights did have a tornado about forty years ago," Mr. Drew said. "But it was a small one and it hit outside of town, so it didn't do much damage."

"Why do some places get tornadoes and others not?" George asked.

"It mostly has to do with location," Nancy said.

"Location?" Hannah said.

Nancy nodded. "Even though tornadoes can form almost anywhere, the central part of the United

States is the perfect place. That's why it's called Tornado Alley."

"And Oklahoma is right in the middle of Tornado Alley," Bess added.

"That's right," Nancy said. "Oklahoma is where the dry air from the polar regions comes in off the Rocky Mountains and meets the warm, moist air coming up from the Gulf of Mexico. When the air masses collide, a tornado can be created."

"I hope they don't plan to collide while we're out there," Hannah said. She shivered again.

Nancy didn't say anything, but she looked out the window to see if there were any dark clouds forming. So far, there weren't. But they were headed right for Tornado Alley, and she knew anything could happen this time of the year.

Early the next morning, after a quick breakfast in St. Louis, Nancy and the others were back on the highway, headed for Oklahoma.

Nancy, Bess, and George spent most of the morning playing cards and talking about things that had been going on in River Heights.

At noon they reached Springfield, Missouri, and stopped for lunch. As they walked toward the entrance to the restaurant, Nancy noticed that there were a lot of dark clouds in the west.

"I wonder if those are the clouds they were talking about in that book," she whispered to Bess and

George so Hannah wouldn't hear her. "They're probably coming in off the Rocky Mountains."

"Let's just hope there's no warm, moist air coming up from the Gulf of Mexico," George said.

The restaurant was crowded, so it was several minutes before the waitress arrived to take their order.

"Sorry it took me so long to get over here, folks," she said. "You can blame it on the atmospheric pressure. It does crazy things to people."

"Yes, it is warm outside," Mr. Drew said.

"It's more than that," the waitress said. "People get nervous and irritable when there are tornado watches out."

"We hadn't heard that," Nancy said. "We're from out of town."

The waitress gave everyone a big smile. "Well, welcome to Tornado Alley, folks. This whole area is under a tornado alert until midnight tonight. That usually means that somewhere around here there's going to be a tornado before morning. Now, then, what would you folks like to eat?"

The speciality of the house was chicken-fried steak with mashed potatoes and gravy, so everyone ordered that.

Nancy thought the food tasted delicious, but she found herself glued to the television set that was mounted on the wall just down from their booth. A local weatherman kept breaking into the regular programming to show the red-shaded tornado-

7

watch area. It covered all of southwest Missouri, where they were now, and the whole state of Oklahoma.

"We'd better hurry," Mr. Drew said suddenly. "We want to get to Medicine Bluff before dark."

Nancy turned to her father and realized he'd been watching the television set himself. He didn't say anything else, but Nancy could tell by his expression that he was worried, too.

"That pie over there sure looks good," Bess said.

"We'll get a piece to go," Nancy said quickly. She knew that Bess would be disappointed to miss dessert.

Two hours later they crossed into Oklahoma, drove through Tulsa and Oklahoma City, and headed toward Medicine Bluff.

Just as they reached Chickasha, a loud clap of thunder shook the RV, and big drops of rain started pounding them.

Hannah screamed.

Mr. Drew suddenly swerved from the right lane into the left lane.

"Dad!" Nancy cried. "Is everything all right?"

"Yes, yes, it's okay. Sorry, everybody," Carson Drew replied. "Hannah's scream startled me."

"Oh, I'm so sorry, Mr. Drew," Hannah said. Her voice was quavering, and Nancy knew she was near tears. "That thunder scared me. I guess it's all that talk about tornadoes."

"We're sorry," Nancy said. "We should have been more thoughtful."

A flash of lightning struck the highway in front of them, and Mr. Drew put on the brakes.

"It's hard to see because of the rain," Mr. Drew said. "I wonder if we should find a place to pull over."

"Turn on the radio, Dad," Nancy said.

"Nancy, we don't have time to listen to music," Mr. Drew said. "We're in the middle of a bad storm."

"It's not music I want to hear," Nancy explained. "It's the weather report."

"Good idea," Mr. Drew said. "Hannah, you do the honors. It's that knob right there."

Hannah's hands were shaking so much that she could hardly tune the radio.

"Stop there, Hannah!" Nancy cried. She had heard a man mention the word *tornado*.

". . . is about a mile wide and is headed toward I-44. Everyone in the path . . ."

"Dad," Nancy said, keeping her voice calm, "we're on Interstate 44." She looked out the window, but the rain was so heavy she could see nothing else.

Nancy knew she had to do something. Beside her, Bess and George sat in wide-eyed silence. The air inside the RV was so oppressive that it was hard to breath. She suddenly remembered that the atmospheric pressure changed dramatically during a tornado.

Suddenly a brilliant flash of lightning lit up the sky.

Nancy gasped. There was a swirling black cloud on the highway. It was coming right toward them.

"Dad! There's the tornado!" Nancy cried. "Pull over! We need to get out of the RV now!"

Carson Drew immediately edged the huge RV onto the shoulder of the highway.

"Get to a ditch!" Nancy shouted. "Curl up and cover your heads!"

Nancy was glad now that Hannah had brought along the book about Oklahoma. She read what people should do if they were caught on the highway during a tornado.

When the RV stopped, Nancy opened the side doors and everyone rushed out into the blinding rain.

To the side of the RV was a deep ditch. Bess and George hurried down into it. Nancy and Mr. Drew each grabbed one of Hannah's arms so she wouldn't stumble and fall.

Above the noise of the rain Nancy heard another noise. It sounded like the roar of a thousand jet planes.

That's it, she thought. That's what they're supposed to sound like.

All of a sudden the rain slackened but not the noise, and the sky filled with flying debris.

"Get down!" Nancy screamed. "Cover your heads!"

As she buried her face in the wet grass, Nancy wondered if they'd get out of this alive.

2

The Green Duffel Bag

"Those are *trees* flying over us!" Bess screamed.

Nancy pushed Bess's head back down into the wet grass. "Don't look!" she shouted.

They might survive being struck by flying objects on other parts of their bodies, Nancy knew, but if something hit their heads, it could kill them.

Suddenly Nancy felt herself being pulled up by the force of the wind.

"Oh, no!" she cried. She had heard stories about people being sucked up into the center of a tornado and then carried for several miles before falling back to earth. Was that going to happen to her now? she wondered.

Desperately Nancy held on to the blades of grass

11

beside her, even though she knew they could easily be ripped from the ground by the power of the tornado.

Against her better judgment, Nancy slowly opened her eyes. She had to see what was going on. The clouds were boiling and churning all around her. The air was still full of debris. The tornado seemed to have a life of its own.

Somehow, over the roar of the wind, Nancy heard a scream. She turned her head slightly. George, too, was floating in the air, with only the thick blades of grass holding her to the earth.

Then, all of a sudden, they both fell back to the ground, and the roaring ceased. The storm had passed.

Nancy lay panting for several seconds, then slowly lifted her head and looked around. They were all still there, but everyone was covered with mud.

George started laughing.

"What's so funny?" Bess demanded, her voice near breaking.

"I couldn't help thinking that if we were mud wrestlers," George explained, "this is what we'd look like."

"Dad, Hannah?" Nancy called. "Are you okay?"

Carson Drew sat up slowly and rubbed the back of his neck. "I don't think there's any damage."

"Me, either," Hannah said, her voice shaking. "But my ears are still ringing from the noise."

"Where did it go?" Bess asked.

Nancy stood up and looked around her. "It must have gone back up into the clouds," she replied. "They do that."

Now everyone else began to stand up slowly.

"We were evidently right on the edge of the tornado," Mr. Drew said. "If we'd been in the middle of it, we wouldn't be here now."

Nancy shivered at that thought.

Suddenly she remembered the RV. It was still beside the road where they had parked it, but some of the windows had been cracked, and Nancy could see a couple of large dents in the side where it had been struck by flying debris. She just hoped it would still run.

Mr. Drew must have been thinking the same thing. "I don't think anyone needs medical attention," he said, "so let's drive on to the farm to see if there's any damage there."

Hannah gasped. "Oh, my goodness!" she cried. "I never thought about that."

Everyone started up the slippery grass bank toward the RV. Once inside, they collapsed into the soft chairs.

"These seats will be filthy," Hannah said.

"We can clean them," Nancy said. "Nothing ever felt so good."

When Mr. Drew started the RV, the engine purred.

"I think it's ready to get out of here, too," Bess said.

Nancy and George laughed.

As Mr. Drew pulled back onto the highway, Nancy stared out the window at the destruction around her. There were trees uprooted everywhere. Power poles had been snapped like twigs.

"Watch out for power lines across the highway, Dad," Nancy said. "They could be dangerous."

"Oh, great," Bess moaned. "We survive a tornado only to be electrocuted."

"I don't see any downed lines ahead of us," Mr. Drew said. "I think they're mostly in the fields."

"Oh, my!" Hannah cried. "Look!"

Everyone turned to see what had drawn Hannah's attention.

Nancy could see a man and a woman wandering around what remained of their front yard. Their large brick house looked as if it had exploded.

"Let's stop, Dad," Nancy said. "Those people may need our help."

When Mr. Drew turned the RV into the driveway and stopped in front of the house, the man and the woman looked at them with dazed eyes.

"The woman's injured," Nancy said. "One side of her face is covered with blood."

"Nancy, there's a first-aid kit under the sink," Mr. Drew said. "Get it and let's see what we can do."

Nancy hurriedly got the first-aid kit and climbed out of the RV. George and Bess were right behind her.

The man and woman just stood where they were. Nancy could see the terror in their eyes.

"I'm Nancy Drew," Nancy said. "My friends and I want to help you."

"It all happened so fast," the man said softly. "We didn't have time to get to the storm cellar."

"I know," Nancy said. She righted a couple of chairs that had been blown out of the house and helped the man and the woman into them. "We got caught in our RV. We took shelter in a ditch," she continued as she began putting bandages on the woman's wounds.

"That's why we're so dirty," Bess said.

"I was almost sucked up into the tornado," George said.

The woman started to cry.

Nancy frowned at George to keep her from telling the rest of the story, because it was obviously upsetting the woman.

Just then Mr. Drew and Hannah walked up and Nancy introduced them.

"We're Joe and Emma Barnes," the man said. "We sure are glad you happened along."

"We're from out of state," Nancy said as she bandaged the woman's head wound. "Hannah inherited a farm from her cousin. That's why we're down here." She hoped that by talking to the woman, she could take her mind off what had happened.

Suddenly Mr. Barnes became agitated and started

looking around frantically. "Where's Billy?" he asked Mrs. Barnes. "Where's Billy?"

Now Mrs. Barnes became upset. "Oh, Joe! Did something happen to Billy?"

"Who's Billy?" Bess asked.

"He's our pride and joy," Mrs. Barnes said.

Mr. Drew looked toward the destroyed house. Nancy knew what he was thinking. How could anyone in there still be alive?

Suddenly a dog barked. Then a yellow head slowly pushed through some of the debris. "Billy!" Mr. and Mrs. Barnes cried together. They seemed to forget about themselves and rushed over to rescue their Labrador retriever.

Just then an ambulance started up the drive. When it stopped, two attendants jumped out. "Is there anyone not accounted for?" the woman asked.

"Everyone's here now. But Mr. and Mrs. Barnes might need some more attending to," Nancy said. "I did what I could."

The other EMS attendant began looking them over. "Well, you stopped the bleeding. Things seem to be all right. But we'll take them to the hospital just in case."

Mr. and Mrs. Barnes thanked everyone again, then Nancy and the others got back into the RV.

As Mr. Drew pulled back onto the road, Nancy looked over her shoulder at the Barneses' house. She couldn't imagine coming home to River

Heights to see their house destroyed like that. She wondered what Mr. and Mrs. Barnes must be thinking, having lost all of their belongings.

Nancy suddenly realized that no one was saying anything. We're probably all thinking the same thing, she decided. How incredibly destructive nature can be.

"I wonder what the farm looks like," Bess said.

Hannah started crying softly. "I was wondering the same thing," she said. "I can't stand to think that it might look like Mr. and Mrs. Barnes's house."

"Isn't this the road?" Mr. Drew asked.

Nancy looked out the cracked side window. Even though it was a country road, it had a street sign at the corner. "Wallace Road," she read.

"That's it," Hannah said as she blew her nose. "My cousin's name was Bertha Wallace."

"You mean they name streets after the people who live on them?" George asked.

Mr. Drew nodded. "It's for 911, I think," he said. "In an emergency it helps the local authorities locate people who live in the country."

The road wasn't much more than a country lane, and it was full of ruts, which caused the RV to bounce up and down.

"What the tornado didn't damage, this road will," Mr. Drew muttered.

"This doesn't look good," Nancy whispered to

Bess and George. She pointed to some of the trees along the side of the road. They were all broken in half.

"There aren't a whole lot of trees around here," George said. "They can't afford to lose too many."

"That must be it!" Hannah shouted. "That must be the farm!"

They all craned their necks to look.

"The house looks okay," Nancy said. "But that barn and those other buildings have seen better days."

"I'm just thankful that the farmhouse is all right," Hannah said. "That's where Bertha's things are."

Mr. Drew turned on to a road that led up to the farmhouse. Limbs from the surrounding trees were scattered across it, which made it even bumpier.

"How did your cousin drive on these roads all the time?" Nancy asked. "This is shaking me to death."

"She didn't drive much these last few years," Hannah replied. "Different people did things for her, including taking her into town. They probably drove pickups."

Mr. Drew pulled the RV up to the front of the house and turned off the engine.

"The house is missing a few shingles, Hannah," Nancy said. "But otherwise it seems to be all right."

"Now what do we do?" George asked.

Hannah started looking in her purse for the key to the front door.

"We need to clear away those tree branches or we

won't be able to get in the front door," Nancy said.

She and Bess and George jumped out of the RV and began clearing a path from the door of the RV to the front door of the farmhouse.

Finally the last of the branches had been moved away, and Hannah could unlock the front door.

Inside, the house had a musty smell from being locked up for several weeks, but it was all very neat.

Nancy tried the light switch. "The electricity works!" she exclaimed. "I'm amazed."

"That's the crazy thing about tornadoes. The damage is so localized," said Mr. Drew. "One house will be untouched, while the house next door will be completely destroyed."

"I'll open some windows," Hannah said.

"We'll do it, Hannah," Nancy answered. She and Bess and George started going through the house, opening up what windows they could, which ended up being only three, because the rest of them were painted shut.

"That should help at least," Nancy said as they walked back into the living room. "Now there's some cross-ventilation."

"I put out some towels for everyone," Hannah said. "You can get that mud off anytime you want."

"Great idea!" everyone chimed in.

After they had all showered and changed clothes, Nancy, Bess, and George decided to check out the damage to the rest of the farm. The three of them stood on the front porch, surveying the scene in front of them. Nancy marveled again at the erratic nature of tornadoes. The farmhouse had barely been touched, but the barn was almost completely destroyed.

Just as they stepped off the porch, Nancy spied something in the top of one of the few trees left standing.

"What is that?" she asked.

Bess and George raised their eyes to where she was pointing.

"It looks like a green duffel bag," George said.

"You're right," Nancy said. "The question is, who does it belong to and how are we going to get it down?"

3

Jimmy Boyd

Nancy turned around. "There must be a ladder here somewhere," she said. "Let's go look."

The three of them started toward a half-destroyed shed just beyond the farmhouse.

"This looks like it used to be a garage," Nancy said. She began pulling at one of the large wooden doors. "Help me with this."

Together, the three friends pulled on the door. Finally they were able to get it open.

"Look! There's an old car inside," Nancy exclaimed. "It survived the storm."

"Just barely," George said. "Those boards from the roof missed it by just a couple of inches."

"There's a ladder," Bess said, pointing.

Nancy saw the end of a ladder sticking out from under some debris. "We can move that easily. Just watch out for rusty nails."

It took the girls several minutes to move the debris, but they were finally able to get the ladder out. It was still useable.

Nancy and George carried it to the tree with the duffel bag.

"George, you and Bess hold it up against the trunk," Nancy said. "I'll climb up and get the bag."

When Nancy reached the top rung of the ladder, she still had to stretch as far as she could to reach the bottom of the bag. It took several tugs to get it out of the branches. Just as she started down the ladder, the bag slipped from her grasp.

"Watch out below!" she cried.

The bag fell to the ground, barely missing Bess's head.

"I could have been killed!" Bess shouted up to Nancy.

"Maybe not," Nancy said. "I don't think there's anything inside it."

George picked up the duffel bag. "You're right, Nancy. It's empty."

"Open it up anyway," Nancy said. "Let's be sure."

George unzipped the duffel bag and pulled it open. "What's this?" She took out several pieces of paper.

"Is anything written on the paper?" Nancy asked.

"I think someone smells a mystery," Bess said with a broad smile.

George and Bess crowded around as Nancy looked at the pieces of paper. Someone had cut out words from magazines and newspapers and pasted them on the paper.

"Ransom notes!" the three of them exclaimed together.

Nancy held up one of the sheets of paper. "Listen to this. 'Get thirty thousand dollars in small bills and take it to the phone booth at the corner of Robertson Street and Norman Drive.'" She looked at Bess and George. "This could be serious."

"What do the other notes say?" Bess asked.

"'Drive south on Main. Stop at the telephone booth at Wilson Lane,'" Nancy read. "'Wait for my call.'"

"Somebody's planning a kidnapping," Bess said. "They must have put these ransom notes inside the duffle bag for safekeeping until they were ready to use them."

"That's possible," Nancy said. She considered for a minute. "Or the kidnapping has already taken place and the tornado blew the duffel bag into the tree before the ransom notes could be delivered."

"I hadn't thought of that," George said.

"Me, either," Bess said.

"I wonder where the tornado picked up the bag," Nancy mused. "If we knew that, we could find out what's really going on." She put the pieces of paper back inside the duffel bag and hurriedly zipped it up. "Let's show this to Dad," she said.

The three friends started toward the house but stopped when they heard a loud engine noise coming up the lane to the house.

Nancy peered in the direction of the noise. "Who could that be?" she asked as an old pickup truck came into view.

"Probably just somebody checking on the farm," George said.

Nancy watched as the old pickup slowly ground its way up the rutted lane. The front windshield was tinted, so she couldn't make out the face of the driver. She put the duffel bag down on the ground behind her, so it would be partially hidden.

The driver stopped the pickup right at the base of the tree and climbed out of the cab. He was about twenty-four or twenty-five, Nancy decided. He was dressed in well-worn jeans, a cowboy shirt, dirty cowboy boots, and a big black hat stained with sweat. Nancy wrinkled her nose. He was also wearing a really strong cologne.

"What are you people doing here?" the man demanded.

"That's just what I was about to ask you," Nancy

said. Not wanting to get into an argument with a total stranger, she made the remark sound like a joke. It didn't work.

"I'm Jimmy Boyd," the man said angrily.

Nancy continued to stare at the man. The name meant nothing to her.

Finally Jimmy blinked. "I worked for Bertha until she died," he continued, still in a sneering tone of voice.

"My friend is Bertha's cousin, and we're here to check out the house," Nancy said after introducing herself.

"I came to check out the barn because she let me store some of my things there," Jimmy continued.

"They're probably all gone," Bess said. "We just got a duffel bag out of this tree."

Nancy shot Bess a look that told her not to say anything else. She didn't want anyone knowing about the duffel bag.

Jimmy Boyd's eyes went to the duffel bag that Nancy had put behind her. "That's mine!" he said.

"No, it's not," Nancy said.

"Hey, I had one just like that in the barn," Jimmy said. "It has some personal letters in it. Now, give it to me!"

"This duffel bag belonged to Bertha," Nancy said. "It has some of her things inside it."

25

"You're lying," Jimmy growled.

"How dare you call our friend a liar!" Bess cried.

"It's okay, Bess," Nancy said, putting a calming hand on her friend's arm. "Just consider the source."

Jimmy Boyd's face turned scarlet with anger. "Don't you talk to me like that," he said as he started toward Nancy.

Nancy stared directly into Jimmy's eyes. She never blinked once.

Jimmy stopped within a few inches of her face. Nancy could almost feel the anger rising off him.

"I want to look inside that duffel bag," Jimmy snapped.

"I can't let you do that," Nancy said. "It doesn't belong to you."

"You'll be sorry," Jimmy spat at her. He looked at Bess and then at George. "You *and* your friends!"

With that, he wheeled around and started back toward his pickup. He started the engine, but instead of driving away, he sped past Nancy, Bess, and George, forcing them to step back in a hurry to keep from getting hit.

"Watch it!" Bess yelled after him.

"Where's he going?" George asked.

Immediately Nancy knew. "Come on!" she cried as she started running after the pickup. "He's headed for the barn."

Jimmy Boyd's pickup was already at the barn

when Nancy, Bess, and George caught up with him.

"You'll have to leave," Nancy said. "This property belongs to Hannah Gruen."

"Who's Hannah Gruen?" Jimmy demanded.

"She's Bertha's cousin, I told you," Nancy replied. "Bertha left Hannah the property in her will."

"Bertha didn't tell me anything about that," Jimmy said.

"Why should she?" Bess demanded.

"I told you," Jimmy said. "I worked for her after I got out of the army." He started to say something else, but then he shook his head and started picking through what was left of the barn.

"What are you doing?" Nancy demanded.

"I'm just trying to see if I can find any of my things," Jimmy replied.

"Well, you could be looting," George said.

Jimmy ignored her and continued picking up stuff.

"Nancy? What's wrong?"

Nancy turned. Hannah and Carson Drew were hurrying toward the barn.

Jimmy Boyd looked up. "Who's that?" he said.

"That's Hannah and Nancy's father," Bess replied. "Mr. Drew is a lawyer."

Nancy noticed that Jimmy looked startled. For the first time since he had been there, she thought she detected a hint of fear in his eyes.

"I see we have company," Mr. Drew said.

"This is Jimmy Boyd," Nancy said. "He said that Bertha let him store some of his things in the barn."

"But I don't believe him," Bess said. George shook her head in agreement.

Jimmy Boyd looked at both Hannah and Mr. Drew as though he was daring them to say something. For several seconds no one spoke.

Then finally Hannah said, "Bertha never mentioned a Jimmy Boyd to me. So as far as I'm concerned, he doesn't belong here."

Nancy knew that Hannah and Bertha hadn't really talked to each other in several years.

Hannah turned to Jimmy. "I'd like you to leave now."

Jimmy threw down a ragged shirt he had been holding in his hands. "I'm going," he said, "but this isn't the last you've heard of Jimmy Boyd."

For several seconds he stared at the duffel bag Nancy was holding, then he got back into his pickup, gunned the engine, and sped off down the road, bouncing over the deep ruts.

"That guy is pretty creepy," George said.

"He's also really angry about something," Nancy said.

"Yes, I think you're right about that," Carson Drew said.

"What's in the duffel bag, Nancy?" Hannah asked.

Nancy opened the bag and pulled out the sheets of paper. "I think they're ransom notes," she replied.

Hannah gasped. "Ransom notes!"

"I wouldn't be surprised if Jimmy Boyd is the kidnapper," Bess said.

"What are you going to do, Nancy?" George asked.

Nancy looked at her father. "I want to pay a visit to the Medicine Bluff Police Department tomorrow, Dad," she said. "I think they'll be interested to know that Jimmy Boyd said this duffel bag belonged to him!"

4

Stolen!

The next morning at breakfast Nancy announced that she was going into Medicine Bluff as soon as she finished eating.

She put down the map of Oklahoma she had been studying. "Who's going with me?" she asked, looking at Bess and George.

"We promised Hannah we'd help her sort through Bertha's belongings this morning. Can't you wait until this afternoon?" Bess asked.

"Bess, we're talking about a kidnapping here," Nancy reminded her patiently. "If it hasn't already happened, then it probably will soon. The police need to know about these ransom notes." Noticing Bess's downcast expression, she added,

"But I'll try to hurry back to help you, too, Hannah."

"I think Cousin Bertha must have kept everything she ever bought," Hannah said as she placed another platter of bacon and eggs on the table. "I've never seen so much stuff in all my life."

"She has so many collectibles all through the house," George said. "I bet they're worth a fortune."

"I need to take the RV into Medicine Bluff this morning to have it repaired," Mr. Drew said to Nancy. "I can drop you at the police station on my way. The mechanic said he'd bring me back out to the farm. I can wait until you've finished talking to the police."

"That's okay, Dad," Nancy said. "I'll use Bertha's car."

"Do you think it still runs?" Hannah asked.

"I'll soon find out," Nancy said. "The keys must be around here somewhere."

"I'm glad that old car wasn't damaged in the tornado," Bess said. "One side of the garage almost fell in on it."

"Well, okay, then, that's settled," Mr. Drew said. He turned to Hannah. "That was a delicious breakfast." He laid his napkin on his placemat. "I'll clear the table. You girls go on and get started."

"Sounds good to me," George said.

They all jumped up from the table, glad to let Mr. Drew clean up.

"I saw some keys hanging on a hook above the

31

sink in the kitchen, Nancy," Hannah said. "They look like car keys to me."

Nancy headed for the kitchen. "If you hear the sound of a car engine, you'll know they worked."

She grabbed the keys, slung the duffel bag over her shoulder, and headed out for the garage.

She was halfway there when she got the feeling that she was being watched. She stopped and glanced around. It was so quiet out in the country. Not a sound. Not even the chirping of a bird or the buzz of an insect. Had the tornado blown them all away? Nancy wondered.

The sky was bright, and there were no clouds in sight. It was such a strange contrast to the day before, when the black, roiling clouds had destroyed houses, uprooted trees, and almost ended their lives.

Nancy shivered, even though it was already warmer than it was this time of the year in River Heights. What's wrong with me? she wondered. She turned a complete circle but saw no one. She decided that she was still a little spooked from the tornado and from the unpleasant meeting with Jimmy Boyd.

Finally she made it to the garage. The car was a dark green sedan and at least ten years old, but it looked to be in pretty good shape, Nancy thought. The tires still had air in them. Now Nancy just hoped the engine started.

The driver's door was unlocked, so she opened it and got in. Nancy was amazed at how little dust was on the seats. She wondered when Bertha had last used the car. There was something very familiar about the smell inside, but Nancy couldn't place it.

Suddenly it hit her. She knew that smell—it was Jimmy Boyd's cologne! He must have been inside the car recently. But Nancy didn't think the car had been driven for a while. Did Jimmy Boyd just sit inside the car? Why would he do that? Nancy wondered.

Nancy quickly locked both doors. Then she realized that she hadn't looked in the seat behind her. Was Jimmy Boyd waiting there for her?

She swallowed hard and slowly turned. The backseat was empty.

Nancy tried two keys on the chain before she finally found the one that fit the ignition.

"Here goes," she whispered as she slowly turned the ignition.

The engine whirred for a couple of seconds, then came to life. The gas gauge registered a half tank.

Nancy shifted into Drive, then slowly pulled out of the garage. Several times she had to maneuver around piles of storm debris. As Nancy passed by the front door of the farmhouse, she honked the horn to let her father and the others know she was on her way.

Nancy bounced along the lane that led to the road, careful to avoid several large branches and not to hit high center. When she reached the main highway, she turned left. She had gone only about two miles when she saw a green sign indicating that Medicine Bluff was only five miles away.

She sped up and was at the city limits in less than ten minutes. She stopped at a service station to ask directions and was told that she'd find police head-quarters right at the edge of the downtown district, about five blocks from where she was. When she got there, she was surprised at how modern the building was. Everything else around it looked much older.

Just inside the front door was an information desk, but no one was sitting at it. Nancy looked around. Suddenly a deputy hurried past her.

"Excuse me," Nancy called to him. She glanced at his name tag. "Deputy Austin, I need to talk to someone about a kidnapping."

The deputy stopped dead in his tracks and turned to face her. "A kidnapping?"

Nancy nodded. "My name is Nancy Drew. And I think either there's already been a kidnapping or there will be one soon."

Deputy Austin gave Nancy a puzzled look. "Well, we haven't had any calls about a kidnapping," he said.

"That's a relief," Nancy said. "That probably means it hasn't happened yet."

"Why do you think there's going to be one?" Deputy Austin asked.

Nancy held up the green duffel bag. "I have the evidence inside this," she said. She started opening up the duffel bag.

"Look, Ms. Drew, I'm really busy," Deputy Austin said. "We had a terrible tornado yesterday, and we're short-handed around here today."

"I know about the tornado. My family and I were caught in it," Nancy said, persisting. "Actually, that's how we found the duffel bag. It was in a tree."

"You were in the tornado?" Deputy Austin said.

Nancy nodded. "Right on the edge of it."

"You were lucky," Deputy Austin said. "Actually, we were all lucky it stayed in open country. Just a few homes destroyed. No one killed. Thank goodness it missed Medicine Bluff." He turned and looked at the door on the other side of the room.

Nancy knew he was trying to make a decision: do what he had originally planned or take a few minutes to listen to her.

"Okay," Deputy Austin finally said. "Come on in here. You can show me what's in the duffel bag."

Nancy followed him into a room that was bare except for a small table and a couple of chairs. Nancy figured that the mirror on the far wall was two-way.

"Is this an interrogation room?" she asked.

"It is," Deputy Austin replied. "How did you know that? You don't look like you've ever been in one before."

"My father's a lawyer," Nancy said.

"You're not from around here?" Deputy Austin asked.

Nancy shook her head. "No. We're from the Midwest." Then she told Deputy Austin about Hannah's inheriting her cousin Bertha's farm.

"Well, let's see what's in the bag," Deputy Austin said.

Nancy unzipped it and pulled out the sheets of paper. She was careful to hold them at the edges, in case the police wanted to dust them for fingerprints.

Deputy Austin scanned the notes for several minutes, then said, "It's probably just a prank."

Nancy looked at him. She couldn't believe her ears. "A prank? Why would anyone make ransom notes for a prank?"

Deputy Austin shrugged. "There's no telling. Kids do the strangest things today."

"I don't think it was a kid," Nancy told him. "I think it was a man named Jimmy Boyd."

The deputy looked surprised. "I thought you weren't from around here. How do you know Jimmy Boyd?"

Nancy told him about Jimmy's visit to the farm the day before when Jimmy had claimed that the duffel bag was his.

"Did you show him what was inside?" Deputy Austin asked.

Nancy shook her head.

"Well, I don't think he would have claimed the bag was his if he had known what was inside," Deputy Austin said. "That would have been kind of dumb, don't you think?"

"Criminals aren't always smart," Nancy retorted.

Deputy Austin smiled. "Well, you have a point there, I guess."

"I think you should bring Jimmy Boyd in for questioning," Nancy told him.

"Look, Ms. Drew, this is just not enough evidence to bring Jimmy in for questioning," Deputy Austin said. "He could say we were harassing him."

Nancy could hardly contain her disappointment. She had been sure that the Medicine Bluff police would take action immediately.

"But what if it's not a prank?" Nancy countered. "What if somebody *is* kidnapped?"

Deputy Austin shrugged. "We'll deal with it then." He looked at the door. "I really do need to get back to what I was doing."

Nancy let out a sigh. "Thank you," she said. She started out of the room. Deputy Austin was right behind her. "I'd just forget this whole business if I were you and enjoy my stay in Medicine Bluff. This place is full of history."

"Okay," Nancy said.

But she had no plans to forget it. The ransom notes were not a joke. Someone around here was planning a kidnapping.

Nancy left police headquarters and stood for a minute on the busy sidewalk. What should she do now? she wondered.

Down the street she spied a sign that said Judy's

Diner. She was suddenly thirsty. She'd go there to get something to drink and to think about her next move. But first, she decided, she'd put the duffel bag back in Bertha's car.

She started down the sidewalk. When she reached the car, she unlocked the trunk and leaned over to put the duffel bag inside.

Just then someone pushed her from behind, causing her to hit her head on the rim of the trunk, lose her balance, and stumble forward. The duffel bag was yanked from her grasp, but Nancy was too dazed to do anything about it.

She quickly pushed herself back to her feet. It had all happened so fast. She doubted if anyone around had seen what happened. Trying to focus, she scanned both sides of the street. Whoever had grabbed the duffel bag had disappeared quickly.

Just then an elderly man walking a dog stopped at the curb.

"Excuse me," Nancy said. "Did you just see anyone with a green duffel bag?"

The man shook his head and walked on.

Was this just a theft? Nancy wondered as she gingerly rubbed the knot on her forehead. Was the bag taken by somebody who thought there was something valuable in the duffel bag. Or was it taken by Jimmy Boyd?

Now the knot on Nancy's head was throbbing.

She headed for the diner to get something to drink and some ice for her forehead.

A waitress was standing at the front of the diner when she entered. She looked about eighteen, the same age as Nancy, and the name stitched on her uniform said *Trudy*. "Wow! What happened to you?" the waitress exclaimed when she saw the bump on Nancy's forehead. "Let me get some ice for that."

Nancy was glad that the diner was almost empty. She didn't want people staring at her. She saw the Seat Yourself sign and took a seat in a rear booth.

The waitress was back in just a few seconds with a glass of water and some ice wrapped in a cloth napkin.

"This ought to help," she said as she handed the ice pack to Nancy. "How in the world did that happen?"

"I'm just clumsy," Nancy said, trying to smile. "I ran into my steering wheel."

The waitress rolled her eyes. "Well, I won't even try to figure out how you managed that. Let me bring you some hot tea."

"That sounds good," Nancy said.

Trudy bustled off toward the kitchen.

Now what? Nancy thought. How can I prevent the kidnapping if I don't have the notes?

Some water from the ice pack dripped onto the table, and Nancy reached for a paper napkin from the holder to wipe it up.

Suddenly Nancy realized that things might not be

so bad after all. She grabbed another napkin and took a pen out of her purse.

She immediately starting writing down as much as she could remember about the ransom notes and the addresses on the maps. She was still writing when Trudy came back.

"Feeling better?" Trudy asked.

Nancy nodded. "This ice really helped."

"This hot tea will make you feel better, too," Trudy said.

Nancy positioned the napkin where Trudy could see it. "Do the names of these streets mean anything to you?" she asked.

Trudy looked. "I think they're all streets around the university," she said. "You know, the University of Southern Oklahoma."

"Thanks," Nancy said. "That's what I needed to know."

Just then a man and a woman came into the diner.

"Uh-oh, I need to go," Trudy whispered. "That's Mr. and Mrs. Connors. They tip really well."

Nancy laughed and took a sip of her tea. It really did make her feel better. That and the fact that she now had a place to start looking for the kidnapper.

5

The Tornado Laboratory

Nancy had another quick chat with Trudy, finished her tea, paid her bill, and said goodbye. "Thanks for all your help," she said.

"My pleasure," Trudy said.

Outside, Nancy hurried along the sidewalk, wishing several times that she had found a parking space closer to the diner. Finally she reached Bertha's car. Before she unlocked the door, Nancy looked around to make sure no one was waiting to spring on her.

But why should they? she thought unhappily. They already have the duffel bag.

Nancy got behind the wheel and pulled away from the curb. As she headed down the street, she remembered Trudy's directions to the university.

Two blocks down from the diner, she came to a stoplight, just as Trudy said she would, and she turned left onto University Drive. Nancy thought she could see the imposing arch that marked the entrance to the University of Southern Oklahoma several blocks away.

Just before Nancy reached it, though, she saw a sign for Robertson Street. That's one of the streets mentioned in the ransom note, Nancy thought.

Quickly she turned onto Robertson Street, which was lined with clothing shops, bookstores, and small restaurants. Nancy noticed several pay phones along the street. She knew a kidnapper could use them to make a call.

The next street she came to was Norman Drive, which was also mentioned in the ransom notes. Nancy knew she was in the area that the kidnapper had written about, but what good did it do her? The streets were crowded with college kids enjoying the late spring day. Could the kidnapper be one of these people? Nancy suddenly wondered.

That would probably leave Jimmy Boyd out of the picture, Nancy thought. He didn't seem the type to be in college. But if he was the kidnapper, why would he write ransom notes with street names that surrounded the university? Was he connected to the university in some other way? Or was it because he knew the area would be crowded with people? That would certainly make his escape easier.

Ahead, Nancy saw Wilson Lane, still another street mentioned in the ransom notes. Nancy realized she was circling the university's campus. Was that what the kidnapper had planned—to confuse the person leaving the money?

Just as Nancy reached the corner of University Drive again, she suddenly braked to a halt. The sign in front of a two-story brick building intrigued her: The University of Southern Oklahoma Tornado Laboratory.

Nancy wondered if anyone in the laboratory could tell her how the duffel bag had got into the tree. Had it blown there from the barn, where Jimmy Boyd said he had stored his bag? Or could it have come from farther away?

She quickly pulled into an empty parking space and got out. She hurried up the sidewalk to the entrance to the building. When she went inside, she expected to see a reception area. Instead, she felt as though she had walked on to the set of a television weather forecast. Lots of college-age men and women hovered around television monitors and weather radar screens.

Nancy stood for a minute, just inside the door, thinking that eventually someone would look up and ask her what she wanted, but after about five minutes, when no one had, she walked over to the nearest desk.

"Excuse me—"

The young man at the desk waved her away with

a brusque "Just a minute. I'm trying to calculate the wind speed of the tornado on this radar screen."

Nancy started to walk away, then stopped to stare at the peculiar image on the screen. There was a little hook at the edge of the huge colored circle. She wondered if the hook was the tornado.

Finally the man swiveled around in his chair to face her. "Now, what did you want?"

"I was just curious about something," Nancy began.

She explained about finding the duffel bag in the tree. "Can someone tell me how far the wind might have blown it?"

Nancy waited for another curt reply, but instead the young man said in a friendly manner, "Tell me the exact location of the tree."

"It's in the front yard of a farmhouse on Wallace Road," Nancy said. "Do you know where that is?"

The young man nodded. "Sure. I've driven past there plenty of times," he said. "My name's Philip, by the way," he added as he started typing instructions to his computer. "What's yours?"

"Nancy Drew," Nancy replied. "I'm visiting. We're down here because our housekeeper, Hannah Gruen, inherited Bertha Wallace's farm."

"Okay, here we go," Philip said. "With the speed of the wind plus the weight of the object, this program can compute possible distances that objects are carried."

After a few moments, Philip doubled-clicked several times, then said, "I'd say that the bag could be carried about twenty miles."

"Wow!" Nancy said.

"Of course, there are a lot of variables," Philip said, "because this is not an exact science."

"What do you mean?" Nancy asked.

"This projection doesn't take into consideration wind gusts or things that might impede the movement of the object," Philip said.

"Like the tree?" Nancy said.

Philip nodded. "The duffel bag could have been picked up just a few feet from where it originally was, blown into the tree, then wedged up there so that the wind couldn't budge it. Tornadoes are notoriously hard to predict. We just do the best we can."

Nancy realized that she was now back to Jimmy Boyd as a possible suspect. She was just about to ask another question, when an older man emerged from a door at the back of the room.

"We have a super cell forming south of town!" he announced. "Let's go!"

All of a sudden the room was filled with an electric feeling. Everyone jumped up at once. They started running around frantically, grabbing equipment off tables and desks. Several people even collided with one another.

Philip snatched a movie camera and a black satchel off the table next to his desk. "See you later!" he called over his shoulder to Nancy as he dashed for the door.

It wasn't long before the room was almost empty. But Nancy noticed that the older man who had made the announcement was still staring at another young man sitting at a computer in a far corner.

"Owens!" the man shouted. "What are you doing here?"

The young man looked up. Nancy could see anger in his face. "I'm compiling data," he replied, never taking his eyes off the man.

Finally the man turned on his heel and stormed out of the room. Why was he so angry at that guy? Nancy wondered. He doesn't seem to be doing anything wrong.

Owens noticed Nancy and stood up. He started walking toward her. "Aren't you going to chase the storm?" he asked.

Nancy blinked. "No. I don't think I'm really supposed to be in here." She paused. "Who was that man?"

"Oh, that was Dr. Johnson," the young man said. "He's the director of the Tornado Laboratory." When he reached her, he added, "Why are you here?"

"I just had a question about how far a tornado could carry an almost empty duffel bag." Nancy extended her hand. "I'm Nancy Drew. I'm visiting from out of town."

"Derek Owens," the young man said with an engaging smile.

"Is that what all those people are going to do?" Nancy said. "Chase a storm?"

Derek nodded. "It's the most important thing in their lives," he replied.

"Why aren't you going with them?" Nancy asked.

"Oh, I plan to. I just had to finish some work on the computer," Derek said. "Now, what was this about a duffel bag?"

"Right after the tornado, my friends and I found a duffel bag in a tree," Nancy explained. "I wanted to find out how it got there."

"Tornadic winds can do some really strange things," Derek said. He looked around the empty room, then turned back to Nancy. "I'll be glad to tell you all about them, but you'll have to come chase the storm with me."

Nancy wasn't sure she wanted to see another tornado, but she wanted to find out about the winds, and Derek seemed willing to talk to her.

"How close will we get to it?" Nancy asked. "We were almost in the middle of a tornado yesterday, and that's enough for me."

Derek grinned. "I understand how you feel, but you'll be safe. We'll only get close enough to collect some data."

"Okay," Nancy finally said.

Derek grabbed his camera and a black satchel.

"Come on, then. Let's see what we can find out."

Nancy hated to admit it, but there was something thrilling about the idea of chasing a storm. Besides, she thought, if Derek could give her information that she could use to solve the mystery of who was planning the kidnapping, it would be worth it.

6

Chasing the Storm

Nancy followed Derek out of the tornado laboratory and around to the back of the building, but when they got to the parking lot, Nancy stopped dead in her tracks. The students were all leaving in cars and vans that each had a bizarre-looking superstructure of instruments on its roof. "They look like they're getting ready to do battle in outer space," she said. "What are those things?"

"Those are VORTEX probe cars," Derek said.

"Vortex probe cars?" Nancy said.

Derek nodded. "VORTEX stands for Verification of the Origins of Rotation in Tornadoes Experiment," he said. "Every six seconds those instruments send atmospheric readings into the memory chips of onboard laptops."

Nancy watched in fascination as the vehicles with their twirling instruments squealed out of the parking lot, heading for the developing storm to the southwest of Medicine Bluff.

When Nancy turned back around, she was surprised that Derek had an angry look on his face as he watched the departing VORTEX probe vehicles. "Shouldn't we hurry?" she asked him. "We're going to lose them if we don't."

Derek turned to face her. For a split second his eyes were vacant, then he suddenly came to life and gave Nancy a big smile. "Oh, don't worry. We'll make it. I was just thinking about something else for a minute there."

Nancy saw that the only other vehicle in the parking lot was a dirty black late-model sedan. There were no VORTEX probe instruments on top of it.

"Ready?" Derek said. He started walking slowly toward the black car.

Puzzled, Nancy followed him. "Why doesn't this car have any weather instruments on top of it?" she asked.

When they reached the car, Derek opened Nancy's door for her, then he got behind the wheel. "Actually, I'm not really one of the weather students, so I'm not an official storm chaser," he said, starting the car. "I used to be. But that was before I had to quit school."

"Oh, I'm sorry," Nancy said.

"It's okay," Derek said. "Things like that happen in life." Derek shrugged. "I had to help support my mom after my dad died. He was a smart guy but a lousy financial planner. There's nothing new about that. It happens all the time."

Nancy didn't know what to say, but she gave Derek a sympathetic smile.

"My dad used to be the director of the tornado laboratory," Derek continued without any prompting. "That's why I like to hang out there. It reminds me of when he was alive." Derek turned to her, and Nancy could see tears glistening in his eyes. "I'm sorry. I still get upset when I talk about it."

"I didn't mean to bring up unpleasant memories," Nancy said. "I know it's hard to lose a parent."

Derek nodded toward the dark clouds ahead of them. "That looks like a good storm," he said, changing the subject. "We should be able to get plenty of pictures."

But then Derek made a sharp turn onto a road, which Nancy thought was taking them away from the storm.

"So, tell me about that duffel bag," Derek said. "What does it look like?"

Nancy looked over her shoulder at the retreating storm. "Why are we going in the other direction?" she asked, changing the subject.

"What do you mean?" Derek said.

"The clouds are behind us," Nancy said. "Shouldn't we be heading toward them?"

"I'm going around the storm so I can see the wall cloud better," Derek replied. "If there's going to be a tornado, that's where it'll develop."

Nancy had to admit that Derek probably knew more about storms than she did, so she'd just have to take his word for it.

"Now, tell me about the duffel bag," Derek said.

"Well, it's just a regular old duffel bag, the kind that athletes carry," Nancy said. "You can buy them almost anywhere."

"What color was it?" Derek asked.

"Green," Nancy replied. But what difference did that make? she wondered.

"What about the weight?" Derek said. "Did it have anything inside it?"

Nancy didn't want to lie to Derek, but she also didn't want to give away her most important information. "Just some stuff," she replied. "It wasn't very heavy."

"What kind of stuff?" Derek persisted.

That funny look was back in his eyes, Nancy saw. She suddenly felt a chill. Why was Derek so persistent about what was inside the duffel bag? she wondered.

Nancy stared out the side window of Derek's car. They were in the middle of nowhere. They hadn't passed one single vehicle. Nancy wondered if the rest of the storm chasers had headed in the opposite direction.

Suddenly Derek speeded up. When Nancy turned to look at him, he was smiling.

"Sometimes I start daydreaming, and I slow down," Derek explained. "We're going to lose the storm if I don't speed up."

When Nancy peered out the front windshield, she could see that they were indeed heading back toward the storm, but this time the clouds had a different formation.

Derek suddenly braked.

Nancy jerked forward in her seat. "What's wrong, Derek?"

"I want to get a picture of that anvil," Derek replied. He grabbed his camera and jumped out of the car. "It's a perfect formation."

Nancy got out and stood to the side of the car, looking up in the direction of Derek's pointed video camera. She was amazed that the cloud really was in the shape of an anvil.

For several minutes Derek took pictures of the storm. Nancy was amazed at how the clouds had started to boil. The wind had picked up, too, and there was the smell of rain, which Nancy realized was the wind-borne smell of raindrops on dirt.

Finally Derek turned to her. "Is your heart pounding?" he asked.

Surprised, Nancy asked, "What do you mean?"

Derek swept the air with his hand. "Look around you, Nancy. Have you ever seen such power? There's nothing stronger than the forces of nature."

Nancy looked up into the sky. Now the clouds were boiling even more and seemed almost unreal. "Well, I agree it's exciting, all right, but I'm not sure I'd say that my heart was pounding."

"Oh, mine is," Derek said.

Derek continued to scan the sky, and Nancy thought he seemed totally oblivious to the approaching danger. Finally she said, "Derek, I think we should leave. I don't want to get caught up in another tornado."

When he didn't respond, Nancy shouted, "Derek!"

Derek's eyes blinked. He looked around, then ran toward the car. "Come on! We need to move!"

Nancy got back into the car and Derek put it in reverse, throwing up gravel as he sped back in the direction they had come.

"Where to now?" Nancy asked. She started to tell Derek that now her heart *had* started pounding.

"Nancy, I'm sorry," Derek said. "I know you probably think I'm weird, the way I get so excited about thunderstorms, but—"

"You don't have to apologize, Derek," Nancy said. "I think it's great."

"What do you feel passionate about?" Derek asked.

"That's easy," Nancy replied. "I love solving mysteries."

"Well, you have a mystery to solve now," he said. "The Duffel Bag Mystery."

"You're right," Nancy said, "but I'm not really having very much luck."

Derek thought for a moment. "Well, it's all about wind force, Nancy. How far could the tornado have carried the duffel bag? There are a lot of scientists who are working on the problem. In fact, I've been thinking about writing a paper on the topic myself. I'm sure it would impress Dr. Johnson. Then maybe he would give me a scholarship, so I could go back to school."

Suddenly Nancy had an idea. "Derek! I know how you can impress Dr. Johnson," she said. "If you can help me solve the mystery of the duffel bag, you'll have done more than just figure out how far the wind carried it, you'll have helped the police solve a crime."

Derek took his foot off the gas pedal, and the car began to slow down. "You're right. Dr. Johnson would have to gve me a scholarship then." He pulled onto the shoulder of the road and stopped. "Nancy, that would be great!" he said. "But you'll have to tell me everything. You can't hold anything back."

Nancy glanced back at the cloud, to make sure they were far enough away, so that slowing down wouldn't put them in harm's way. It seemed safe enough.

"There were several sheets of paper in the duffel bag," Nancy explained. "I think they're ransom notes."

Derek got a puzzled look on his face. "Ransom notes? How do you know they're ransom notes?"

As best as she could remember, Nancy related their contents to Derek. "Someone pushed me and stole the duffel bag, just after I left the police station," Nancy said. "I don't have the notes anymore, but right after it happened, I wrote down what I could remember."

"You went to the police?" Derek asked.

Nancy nodded.

Derek considered that information, then asked, "Do the police know what the ransom notes say?"

Nancy nodded again. "The deputy I spoke to does, but he thinks they're a joke. I'm sure he's forgotten all about them by now."

Derek twisted his mouth as he thought about what Nancy had said. "That's good."

Nancy gave him a puzzled look.

"What I mean is, if the police solve this mystery before I do, then I won't get the credit," Derek said.

"That's true," Nancy agreed.

Derek pulled back on to the highway. For several minutes they rode in silence. Finally Derek turned to Nancy. "I've been doing some calculating in my head," he said. "I think that the duffel bag probably came from somewhere very close to the tree where you found it."

"Really?" Nancy said.

That's strange, she thought. Back at the Tornado Laboratory, Philip had used a computer program to calculate that the duffel bag could have come from as far as twenty miles away. Was Derek really so good at this that he could do it all in his head?

Who was right? Nancy wondered.

7

Another Suspect

"I have an idea who the kidnapper could be," Nancy said.

Derek gave her a surprised look. "Already? For someone from out of town, you sure work fast. Who is it?"

"A man showed up at the farm right after we arrived," Nancy explained. "When he saw the duffel bag, he said it belonged to him. Now, after what you just said, that makes sense."

Suddenly the car swerved, but Derek straightened it after a couple of seconds.

"What happened?" Nancy gasped.

"Nothing, I just . . ." Derek took a deep breath

and slowed down the car. "I don't know. I just felt funny all of a sudden."

"Do you want me to drive, Derek?" Nancy asked. "I don't mind. You can tell me where to turn."

"No, that's okay. I'm all right now," Derek said. "It's just that sometimes I get these really awful headaches."

Nancy wasn't sure if Derek really was all right, but she decided not to press the issue. "Do you know someone named Jimmy Boyd?" she asked.

"Sure," Derek said. "Medicine Bluff's not that big."

"Do you think he could be a kidnapper?" Nancy continued.

Derek shrugged. "I know he was in the army, and I think he got into trouble there."

"Really?" Nancy said. "What sort of trouble?"

"I don't know," Derek replied. "But as far as I'm concerned, if you've done something wrong once, you could do something wrong again."

"That's often the case," Nancy agreed.

"Did you tell the police you suspect Jimmy?" Derek asked.

Nancy considered whether to reveal everything to Derek and decided not to. "As I said, the police weren't very interested in what I had to tell them," Nancy replied. "So I didn't get that far in my story."

"Actually, it's probably better that they don't know about him," Derek said. "They might start tailing him and then he'd lie low for a while."

"You could be right," Nancy said. "If he thinks no one is onto him, maybe he'll attempt the kidnapping."

"He's probably the one who hit you over the head and took the duffel bag," Derek said.

"He'd do something like that," Nancy agreed. "He probably thinks that without the evidence there's no way anyone can prove anything."

But he's wrong, Nancy thought. I'll be right there when he makes his move.

Up ahead, Nancy saw a VORTEX probe car pulled to the side of the road. One of the storm chasers was changing a tire.

"Shouldn't we stop?" Nancy said. "They might need our help."

Derek slowed the car and pulled off behind the VORTEX probe car.

The two storm chasers looked up and waved.

"It's Charles Stanley and Brent Smith," Derek said.

Derek and Nancy got out and started toward the car.

"You guys all right?" Derek called to them.

"Yeah. Just a flat tire," one of the guys said. He stood up and dusted off his hands. "If I can't find a job with a weather bureau after I graduate, I can always get one at a tire place."

"Who's your friend, Derek?" the other guy asked.

"This is Nancy Drew," Derek replied. "She's visiting."

The guys introduced themselves to Nancy.

"Are you a long way from home?" Charles asked. "Are you here to chase storms?"

Nancy smiled. "Not really," she replied. "Our housekeeper inherited some land. We came down on business."

"Hey! Didn't I see you earlier at the Tornado Laboratory?" Brent asked.

Nancy nodded. "I was just curious about what you did," she said. "We were right on the edge of that big tornado yesterday, so when I saw the Tornado Laboratory, I thought it would be interesting to find out more about how tornadoes form."

"I took her out and showed her the storm," Derek added.

"We got some great measurements during the formation," Brent said. "Unfortunately, it fizzled out."

"Unfortunately?" Nancy exclaimed. "Aren't you glad it didn't form, so it wouldn't do any damage?"

"Oh, well, of course we don't want it to do any damage," Charles said. "We just like to study the formations so we can educate the public better about tornadoes."

"That's a very good idea," Nancy agreed.

"Come on, Charles," Brent said. "We need to get back to the tornado laboratory."

"Derek got some great shots of the storm, too," Nancy told them. "We'll probably see you there."

Charles and Brent both gave her funny looks.

Nancy figured it was because they didn't think Derek had any business at the laboratory. They got back into their VORTEX probe car and pulled on to the highway.

Derek turned to Nancy. "Why did you tell them that? Did you see how they looked at me?"

"Yes, I saw, and I think it's too bad," Nancy said.

"I know as much about tornadoes as they do, Nancy, but they're part of the program, and I'm not," Derek said. "It makes a big difference."

"Well, if you can solve this mystery using your knowledge of tornadoes, then I'm sure Dr. Johnson will be impressed," Nancy said. "Maybe something good will come from that, Derek."

"I'd like to believe that, Nancy," Derek said. "My life would really change if it were true."

"Then what are we waiting for?" Nancy said. "Let's get started."

They got back into Derek's car.

"Where do you want me to drop you?" Derek asked.

"My car's parked at the tornado laboratory. Take me there," Nancy said. "I should be getting back to the farm, because they'll all be wondering what happened to me, but tonight I'll think about how we can catch Jimmy Boyd before he kidnaps anyone."

"That sounds good to me. I'll leave the mystery solving to the expert," Derek said. "You just tell me what I'm supposed to do, and I'll do it."

It didn't take them long to reach the tornado laboratory. Derek pulled up in front and let Nancy out beside her car.

"Can we meet somewhere tomorrow," Nancy asked, "so we can talk about what we're going to do?"

"How about the Student Union at eleven o'clock?" Derek said.

"Okay. I'll be there," Nancy said. "That should give me plenty of time to take care of anything Dad might have planned. If I get there a little early, I'll just look around until you arrive."

"See you," Derek said.

Nancy got out and watched as Derek drove down the street. She had expected him to go back into the Tornado Laboratory, but he headed in the opposite direction. I wonder where he's going, she mused.

Nancy got into Bertha's car and pulled away from the curb. It was almost five o'clock. She was sure everyone would be wondering where she was.

Nancy was already in the center of downtown Medicine Bluff, passing the diner, when she suddenly decided to stop to talk to Trudy. Nancy wanted to find out more about Jimmy Boyd and Derek Owens. She had a feeling that Trudy might be able to tell her what she wanted to know.

There was an empty parking space in front of the floral shop next to the diner, and Nancy pulled the car into it. It occurred to her, as she alighted, that

Trudy might not be working now, but as Nancy approached the front door, she saw Trudy through the window. Luck was with her.

Trudy saw Nancy the minute she came through the front door.

"Hello again!" Trudy cried. She ran toward her as though Nancy was a long-lost friend. "I was hoping you'd come back. There's someone who wants to meet you."

Nancy was puzzled. She couldn't imagine who it would be.

Trudy took Nancy's hand and led her toward a back table. A girl about their age was sitting huddled in the corner. She had her hands around a mug of coffee, as though she were trying to keep them warm.

"This is Mary Harvey," Trudy said to Nancy.

"Hi," Nancy said. "I'm Nancy Drew."

"Oh, hi," Mary said. "I'm so glad you came back."

That's strange, Nancy thought. Why would she say that? She sat down in the booth across from Mary. "Did you have something you wanted to ask me?"

Mary looked around to see if anyone else was watching them. There were just a few other customers in the diner, but they were sitting up toward the front.

Trudy smiled. "No one can hear you, Mary," she said.

Mary still leaned forward, though, so she could whisper to Nancy. "I went to police headquarters this afternoon to see if anyone had turned in a duffel bag."

Nancy suddenly felt goose bumps on her skin. "A duffel bag?" she said.

Mary nodded and looked around the diner again. She leaned even closer to Nancy. "Our mobile home was destroyed by the tornado. I couldn't find the duffel bag in the debris, so I'm sure the tornado must have picked it up and carried it somewhere." Mary paused for a few seconds as she looked intently into Nancy's eyes. "The police told me that a girl had been in earlier, telling them that she had found a duffel bag that fit the description of the one I lost. They described you to me, and then I described you to Trudy. She knew right away who I was talking about."

Nancy looked over at Trudy, whose eyes were sparkling.

"Isn't this just too much?" Trudy said. "Can you believe it?"

It really was hard for Nancy to believe. "Describe the duffel bag you lost," she said to Mary.

Mary gave a perfect description of the duffel bag that Nancy had found in the tree.

"Do you have it with you?" Mary asked.

Nancy took a deep breath. If the duffel bag belonged to Mary, how could she explain the ransom notes inside it? Mary didn't seem like the type of person who would kidnap someone. "Not anymore," she replied.

Trudy gasped.

"Somebody stole it from me," Nancy replied. "That's really how I got that bump on my head."

Trudy's mouth dropped open. "You didn't tell me that, Nancy!"

"I'm sorry, Trudy. That's one of the reasons I stopped back," Nancy said. "I was going to ask for your help in solving the mystery."

Trudy sat down next to Nancy. "I'm not supposed to do this, but I need to think."

Suddenly Mary scooted across the seat and ran toward the front of the diner.

"Mary!" Trudy shouted.

It took a few seconds for Trudy to get up from the seat, so that by the time Nancy started toward the door, Mary was no longer in sight.

Nancy left the diner, but as she looked up and down the street, she couldn't see Mary anywhere.

"Where did she go?" Trudy asked.

Nancy shook her head. "I don't know. She's completely disappeared!" She turned to Trudy. "Do you know anything about her?"

Trudy shook her head. "No. I'm new in town. I've never seen her before today."

8

A New Twist

"You always attract excitement, Nancy," Bess said as Mr. Drew steered Bertha's car down the rutted lane toward the highway. "Life is certainly never dull when we're around you."

"Well, I like that," Hannah said, giving Bess a look that made everyone laugh.

"I didn't mean I was bored yesterday, Hannah," Bess explained quickly. "I enjoyed helping you sort through Bertha's things."

"What you mean is that you enjoyed eating half of the lemon meringue pie that Hannah made," George interjected. "That took up most of your time."

"It did not!" Bess protested.

Nancy laughed. "It really doesn't matter now," she said. "You're going with me today, and that's what's important."

"Are you sure you'll be able to get back to the farm?" Mr. Drew asked. "I don't like leaving you in Medicine Bluff without any transportation."

"We'll be fine, Dad," Nancy assured him.

"I'm sorry the RV is still in the shop," Mr. Drew continued to explain. "Hannah and I have too many things to take care of or you could have Bertha's car again."

"I'm sure Derek will bring us home," Nancy said.

"Tell us about him, Nancy," Bess said. "Does he have any friends?"

Nancy rolled her eyes. "Bess, he's just helping me solve the mystery," she said. "This isn't a date."

"But he does sound interesting, Nancy," George said.

"Well, he seems like a really nice guy," Nancy said. "He'd still be in college, but he had to drop out to help support his mother. I think that bothers him a lot."

"I can't wait to meet him," Bess said.

"There's the bank up there, Mr. Drew," Hannah said. She pointed up the street. "I'm just glad they have a branch of the bank that I use at home."

"That's getting to be really common," Mr. Drew said. "It certainly is convenient."

Mr. Drew pulled into the bank's parking lot and found an empty space next to an old pickup.

"That looks just like Jimmy Boyd's," Nancy said.

"A lot of people drive pickups around here," Mr. Drew said. "This one doesn't necessarily belong to Jimmy."

Nancy knew her father was right, but she had a feeling that she was, too.

"Hannah and I will be only a few minutes. Then we can drive you to the Student Union," Mr. Drew said. "The manager of the bank said he'd have the papers ready for Hannah to sign. I told Hannah I'd look over them first."

"We want to go inside, too," Nancy said. She looked at Bess and George. "My legs are cramped back here. I need to stretch."

"Oh, that's a great idea, Nancy," Mr. Drew said, winking at her. "And while you're inside, why don't you look around to see if you can locate Jimmy Boyd?"

Nancy grinned. She knew better than to try to fool her father. "Thanks for suggesting it, Dad," she teased him.

The five of them headed toward the front entrance to the bank. Nancy suddenly wondered what she'd say if Jimmy Boyd saw her. Would he be as angry as he was yesterday? she wondered. She certainly hoped not. She didn't want an unpleasant scene in the bank.

Mr. Drew held the door open for Hannah. The others followed, but Nancy stopped just inside.

"I don't believe it!" she gasped.

She grabbed Bess and George and pulled them behind a marble pillar.

Mr. Drew and Hannah gave them a curious look but proceeded to one of the teller windows. Nancy was glad that they were used to her sometimes mysterious behavior. She didn't want anyone to call attention to her now.

"What's wrong?" George whispered. "You look as though you've seen a ghost."

"Well, she's not a real ghost," Nancy replied, "but she certainly disappeared on me yesterday."

George peered around the corner. "Oh! Is it the girl you told us about last night?" she whispered. "Mary Harvey?"

"Yes. She's the first teller," Nancy replied. Suddenly Nancy clamped a hand over her mouth. "Oh, no!"

"Jimmy Boyd!" Bess whispered as the man standing in front of Mary's teller window turned just enough so that the three of them could see his face. "You were right, Nancy. That was his pickup."

"This could just be a coincidence," George said. "Jimmy has to go to the bank like everybody else."

"I don't think so," Nancy said. "Look. He and Mary are arguing about something."

70

"Let's get closer to them," Bess suggested. "We can hide behind that potted tree."

"Good idea, Bess," Nancy said.

They moved from behind the pillar to the potted tree as stealthily as they could, but even though they were closer to the teller's windows, it was still impossible to hear what Jimmy and Mary were saying.

"Is there a problem here?"

Nancy and her friends whipped around. They were face-to-face with a security guard.

"No, we were just admiring this beautiful tree," Nancy hurriedly explained. "What kind is it, anyway?"

"I think it would look really neat in our apartment, don't you, Nancy?" George said.

"Oh, definitely," Nancy replied. She felt one of the leaves.

"I know just where to put it, too," Bess said. "It will go so well in that empty corner."

Nancy could tell by the way the guard was looking at them that he didn't know whether to believe them or not.

Just then Jimmy Boyd wheeled around angrily and began stalking out of the bank.

"Well, maybe this tree wouldn't work in our apartment after all," Nancy said. She grabbed hold of Bess and George and they started out of the bank, but they stayed far enough behind Jimmy so that if he turned around they could duck behind one of the writing tables.

But Jimmy was obviously so angry about something that it never occurred to him to turn around.

"Shouldn't we follow him?" George asked.

"How? We have to wait for Hannah and Dad," Nancy said. "Oh, what I wouldn't give to have my car here in Medicine Bluff now."

"But what if he gets away?" Bess asked. "What if he kidnaps somebody?"

Nancy thought for a minute. "I don't think he's going to do anything without Mary," she finally said.

"What do you mean?" George asked.

"I think that may be what they were arguing about," Nancy replied. "They're probaby in this together."

"You mean they're both planning to kidnap somebody?" Bess said.

"Yes, I do," Nancy said, "and I don't know why I didn't think of this sooner."

"Think of what?" George asked.

"What better place to find out who has a lot of money than in a bank?" Nancy said.

"Of course!" Bess said.

At that moment Hannah and Mr. Drew came out of the bank.

"I thought we'd lost you," Mr. Drew said. "One minute you were in the bank, and when I turned back around you were gone."

"Jimmy Boyd *was* in the bank, Dad," Nancy told her father. "He was arguing with a girl I met yesterday."

She quickly reminded him about Mary Harvey and her missing duffel bag.

"What is this with duffel bags?" Mr. Drew asked. "Does everyone in Medicine Bluff own one?"

Nancy laughed. "I'm beginning to think they do." She looked at her watch. "Can you drop us at the Student Union now, Dad?" she asked. "Derek's probably wondering where we are. I can hardly wait to tell him what happened this morning."

They got back into Bertha's car, and with Nancy giving directions headed for the university.

When they reached the Student Union, Mr. Drew pulled up under the portico. Nancy, Bess, and George got out, and hurried through the front door of the Student Union.

"Where were you supposed to meet Derek?" Bess asked.

"We didn't actually decide on a specific place," Nancy replied. She stopped and looked around. "I had no idea the Student Union would be so big," she said. "He could be anywhere."

"Hi," Bess said.

Nancy turned to look at her. A couple of guys with book bags slung over their shoulders were just passing. They had big grins on their faces.

Nancy shook her head in amusement. "We'd bet-

73

ter keep moving," she said to George, "before Bess gets us in trouble."

"That's the truth," George said.

Bess rolled her eyes at them.

They headed across the atrium toward a food court. "Maybe Derek's in here," Nancy said. "This would be a good place to wait for someone."

There were about twenty different fast food concessions circling a huge patiolike courtyard, but Nancy couldn't spot Derek anywhere among the crowd of animated students.

"There are probably some study areas upstairs," George said. "Maybe he just wanted to wait someplace quiet."

"Let's check it out," Nancy said.

They left the food court and, after studying the union directory, took an escalator to the second floor.

Just as they reached the top, Nancy said, "There he is!"

"Who's that girl he's talking to?" Bess asked.

"I don't know," Nancy said. "Derek!" she called.

When Derek turned toward them, he gave Nancy a sheepish grin.

When the three of them reached Derek and the girl, Nancy introduced Bess and George.

"This is Candace," Derek said. "She lost her books and I found them."

"Lucky for you," George said to Candace. "Books can be expensive to replace."

"That is so true," Candace said. "I left them on that study desk over there while I went downstairs, and when I came back they were gone."

"That's strange," Nancy said. She turned to Derek. "Where did you find them?"

"Somebody had dropped them in the stairwell," Derek replied. "I don't like escalators or elevators," he explained. "I always use the stairs."

Nancy felt like laughing. She had never heard such a lame excuse in her life. She wondered if Derek had taken the books, then told Candace he had found them, just so he could talk to her.

"Candace was telling me how she likes to spend her free time," Derek said. "Can you believe that she actually hikes Big Bear Canyon all by herself?"

"Where's Big Bear Canyon?" Nancy asked. "We're just visiting here."

"It's about ten miles outside Medicine Bluff," Candace volunteered. "Not many people go there. It's too isolated. But that's what I like about it." She sighed. "I don't live on campus. My parents thought that would be a waste of money, since we live right here in town. So Big Bear Canyon gets me away from them. They're divorced, but you'd never know it from the way they argue about me on the telephone every day."

"We'll have to hike the canyon together sometime," Derek said. "I love stuff like that."

For several minutes Candace described in great detail the different trails in the canyon and which ones were the most dangerous. What she told them was interesting, but Nancy wanted to talk to Derek about the case, so she was glad when Candace finally said, "You were so sweet about my books, Derek. I can't thank you enough. I'm sure I'll see you around." Turning to Nancy, Bess, and George, she added, "It was nice to meet you. I hope you enjoy the rest of your stay in Medicine Bluff."

"Thanks," Nancy, Bess, and George said in unison.

Nancy waited until Candace had disappeared around a corner, before she tried to talk to Derek. Then she said, "We have some very interesting news for you."

Derek turned to her. "I'm listening," he said.

Nancy told him about Mary Harvey and her missing duffel bag. Then she told him about seeing Mary Harvey talking to Jimmy Boyd in the bank.

"Nancy thinks they're in it together," Bess said.

"Really?" Derek said.

George nodded. "And nobody has solved more mysteries than Nancy Drew."

Nancy felt herself blushing. "George, Bess, you're embarrassing me," she said.

"Don't be embarrassed, Nancy," Derek said. "Be proud."

"I think we should tail them," Bess said. She turned to Nancy. "That's what we'd do if we were at home."

"It would be easy in River Heights," Nancy said. "I could use my car." She turned to Derek. "Could we all go in yours, Derek? Our RV is still being repaired, and Dad and Hannah have Bertha's car today. We don't have any way of getting around."

Derek looked at his watch. "Not now," he said. "I have something else I need to take care of."

Nancy couldn't believe her ears. What could be more important than stopping a kidnapping? she wondered.

9

A Confrontation

"I have to go to the tornado laboratory," Derek explained. "I want to talk to Dr. Johnson again."

"Now?" Nancy said. "Couldn't it wait?"

Derek shook his head. "It's important, Nancy."

"This is important, too, Derek," Nancy protested. If only she had her own car here, Nancy thought, feeling frustrated. Then she wouldn't have to worry about depending on Derek. "We need to stop Jimmy Boyd and Mary Harvey from kidnapping someone."

"I won't be long," Derek promised. He had already started walking away from them, so Nancy knew there was no use in trying to stop him. "I won't be long," Derek repeated.

"We'll be in the food court," Nancy called to him. "Meet us there."

She hoped Derek had heard her, because he turned the corner before she had finished talking.

"I'm glad you said that, Nancy," Bess said. "I'm getting hungry, and I didn't want to sit up here and wait for him."

"You know, Derek seems kind of flaky to me," George said.

"Well, he's got his problems, all right," Nancy agreed, "but if he can help me solve this mystery, it may help him get back into school."

The three of them took the escalator down to the first floor and headed to the food court. The crowd had thinned out considerably since they had been there earlier, so they had a good choice of seats.

"There's so much to choose from," Bess said as she began scanning the huge menus that were hanging above the counters of the various eateries. "I'll never be able to make up my mind."

"I just want a cup of soup and a salad," Nancy said.

"I think I'm going to have a hamburger with all of the trimmings," George said. She started walking toward Western Burgers.

"I'll wait here, while you and George get your food," Nancy said to Bess. "Somebody needs to watch our things."

"We won't be long," Bess said, and hurried away toward Little Italy.

Nancy looked around the food court. Being in the Student Union reminded her of Ned Nickerson, her boyfriend, who was in college. And that made her wonder what Ned was doing at this very moment. She wished they were together now, talking about the duffel bag mystery over a hamburger and fries.

"Mmm, this looks so good."

Nancy came out of her reverie to see Bess carrying a plate piled high with spaghetti and meatballs and two slices of garlic toast.

"You're right," Nancy said. "It does look good."

"They have such huge hamburgers here!"

Nancy looked up to see George returning with one of the biggest hamburgers she had ever seen.

"What is that?" Nancy said.

"It's called the Oklahoma Burger," George replied. "They had a Texas Burger, but it's smaller."

Nancy laughed. "I've heard about the rivalry between Texas and Oklahoma," she said, "but I didn't know it extended to the size of hamburgers."

"Evidently," George said as she sat down. "And I'm glad, too," she added as she took a big bite.

Nancy stood up. "Well, I think I still want soup and a salad. I'll be back in a minute."

When Nancy reached Super Salad, at the other end of the food court, she considered her choices.

"I'll take a garden salad and a cup of . . . well, the southwest barley soup looks good," Nancy told the girl at the counter.

"That's our specialty," the girl said. She rang up Nancy's order and smiled when Nancy handed her the correct change. "People have been giving me large bills all day and I don't have much change left."

The girl ladled out a cup of soup, took a garden salad out of the refrigerator, and put it all on a tray. "Enjoy," she said as she handed the tray to Nancy.

"Thanks," Nancy said. She headed back toward the table where both Bess and George were totally engrossed in their food.

Nancy tasted the soup. It was good.

After a couple of minutes George said, "I think I want some dessert."

"Check out that ice cream over there," Bess said, pointing.

"I give this Student Union an A plus for food," George said, getting up. "I could eat all of my meals here."

"Me, too," Bess said.

They headed toward Sweet Stuff to get a couple of ice-cream cones. When they returned, Nancy had finished her soup and salad.

Nancy dabbed her mouth with her napkin and checked her watch. Derek had been gone thirty minutes. She thought he'd be back by now. What could he be doing? she wondered.

Maybe Derek is more focused on getting back into school than he is on helping me solve this mystery, she finally decided. I can understand that,

Nancy told herself. But she was still puzzled about why Dr. Johnson would be so upset with Derek if the only reason he dropped out of school was to help at home after his father died. Was there some other reason? she wondered.

Derek really had been gone too long for just a short conversation. Something must have gone wrong. Nancy hoped that Derek hadn't gotten so upset about something that he left campus without remembering what they were planning.

Nancy stood up. "I'm going to go look for Derek," she announced. "Wait here in case he comes back while I'm gone."

"Okay," Bess and George said.

Before she left the Student Union, Nancy checked a campus map. If she were driving, she'd have to circle the entire campus, as she had done the day before, but walking, she realized that the tornado laboratory was just three buildings south of the Student Union. She could be there in just a few minutes.

She decided on the route that seemed the most likely, thinking that if Derek were on his way back, she'd meet him, and then they could walk back to the union together.

Nancy exited the Student Union on the south, rather than going out the main entrance, and found herself in a large courtyard. She was amazed at how well landscaped the campus was, given the relatively arid nature of the region. There were trees and shrubs everywhere, and from time to time she came upon hidden garden spots that were very inviting because of the cool shade they offered.

Finally she reached the tornado laboratory, but instead of going into the building through a rear entrance, she decided to go around to the front, as she had done the day before, so she would be in the main lab area.

When she opened the door, a couple of people looked up momentarily, but the rest of them kept their eyes glued to the computer screens in front of them.

Nancy headed toward the back of the room, toward the door through which Dr. Johnson had come the day before.

It led to a corridor that was lined with what Nancy thought might be offices, but all of the doors were closed. She had just turned around to go back into the main lab area to ask if anyone had seen Derek, when she heard angry shouting coming from somewhere down the hall and around the corner.

She started walking in the direction of the voices.

When she turned a corner, she could see an open door at the end of the corridor.

As she approached it, she recognized Derek's voice. But it was a Derek she didn't know.

"You're a sorry excuse for a director!" Derek screamed. "The university should fire you. You're stupid, and you don't know half of what I know about tornadoes!"

Nancy reached the door to Dr. Johnson's office just as the director shouted, "Get out of here! Don't let me ever see you in the tornado laboratory again or I'll have you arrested!"

"You just try it and I'll—"

"Derek?" Nancy said.

Derek whirled around, and Nancy saw that his face was so contorted with anger that a vein in his temple was pulsing.

"Is this young man a friend of yours?" Dr. Johnson demanded of Nancy.

"Yes, he is," Nancy said.

"Then get him out of here before I call the police," Dr. Johnson said.

Nancy touched Derek on the arm. "Come on," she said. "We have things that we need to do."

Nancy was actually surprised when Derek almost let her pull him out of Dr. Johnson's office. They had gone only a few feet when Dr. Johnson slammed the door behind them. Nancy felt Derek tense, but she didn't let go of his arm.

Instead of going back through the laboratory, Nancy saw an Exit sign at the end of the corridor and headed toward that. The bright sunlight blinded her as they exited, and she realized that this was the rear entrance that she had seen before.

Nancy waited until they had reached one of the

hidden gardens before she stopped. She opened her mouth to speak, but Derek stopped her with "Why were you spying on me?"

The accusation stunned Nancy. "I wasn't spying on you. I was worried about you."

"Why?" Derek demanded.

"Why?" Nancy asked incredulously. "You said you'd be back in a few minutes. You weren't."

Derek took a deep breath. "I'm sorry."

Nancy nodded in the direction of the tornado laboratory. "What was that all about?" she asked.

"I'm just angry because Dr. Johnson still won't listen to my ideas about storm chasing," Derek said. "They're doing it all wrong. They'll never get any good data if they don't change the way they collect it."

"Derek. You just have to realize that some people are like that," Nancy said. "They don't like it when other people, especially younger people, suggest changes."

"I guess you're right, Nancy," Derek said. He sighed. "I'm sorry. I just lost my temper, and I shouldn't have. It won't do me any good."

"That's true," Nancy told him.

"Well, at least I got it off my chest," Derek said, giving her a big smile, "and now I'm ready to solve the mystery."

"Good," Nancy said. She grabbed his arm and they hurried back to the Student Union at a fast clip.

They found Bess and George standing in front of China Wok.

"We were just admiring the scenery," Bess explained.

Nancy laughed. "Well, come on, you two. It's time to go," she said. "Derek's here now, so let's see if we can find Jimmy Boyd and Mary Harvey and try to stop a kidnapping."

10

Caught!

Derek knew where Jimmy Boyd lived, so they drove from the Student Union to a trailer park on the outskirts of Medicine Bluff. Jimmy's mobile home looked as if it had seen better days. The yard around it was full of tall weeds.

"What a dump!" Bess whispered.

"Maybe Jimmy can't afford anything else," Nancy said as she surveyed the dwelling.

"I'm glad we're all together," George said. "I'd hate to be out here by myself."

Derek turned to Nancy. "You're the detective. What do we do now?"

"We wait," Nancy replied. "His pickup is here, so

he's probably home. I have a feeling we won't have to wait long."

But three hours later they were still there.

"It's starting to get dark," Bess said. "Pretty soon, we won't be able to see anything."

"Look!" Nancy whispered.

Jimmy was coming out the front door of the trailer.

"Do you think he'll see us?" asked George.

Nancy had forgotten to ask Derek if Jimmy might recognize his car, but they were parked behind some bushes, so she didn't think he'd pay attention to it.

In fact, Jimmy didn't even look in their direction as he headed toward his pickup. After several unsuccessful attempts to start the engine, it finally turned over, and Jimmy drove out the entrance to the trailer park.

Derek started his engine but waited until they were on the highway to turn on his lights.

"Do you see him?" Bess asked.

"Those are his taillights up ahead," Derek said. "I'm sure of it."

"I wonder where he's going?" George asked.

"We'll soon find out," Nancy replied. She was hoping that Jimmy would try something tonight.

They soon came to a more populated part of Medicine Bluff, so it was easier to stay closer to the pickup.

"His blinker's on," Nancy said. "He's turning."

"I'm amazed that old pickup even has a blinker," George said.

"Do you think they'd kidnap somebody tonight?" George said. "Should we get the police?"

"No!" Derek cried.

His outburst startled Nancy. Why was Derek so nervous all of a sudden? she wondered. "Is something wrong?" she asked.

"I've just never done anything like this before," Derek said. "I just hope everything goes all right."

"Don't worry about it," Bess said. "Nancy knows what she's doing. She's solved a lot of mysteries over the years."

"So I've heard," Derek said. He sounded angry.

There *is* something wrong, Nancy decided, but now wasn't the time to find out what it was.

"He's stopping up ahead," Bess said.

"Slow down, Derek," said Nancy. "We don't want him to suspect that we're following him."

Derek pulled the car over to the curb and stopped.

Instead of going into any of the houses, though, Jimmy simply honked.

"That is so rude!" Bess said. "I'd never go out with a guy who did that."

In a few minutes Mary Harvey came bounding out the front door of a white clapboard house and ran to the pickup. Nancy remembered that Mary said her mobile home had been destroyed in the tornado and guessed she was staying with relatives. She was barely inside before Jimmy Boyd took off down the street.

"He's in a hurry," Nancy said. "This doesn't look good."

Derek pulled back into the street and began following the pickup again.

"You remember what those ransom notes said, Nancy," George said. "The person delivering the money had to be at those pay phones at very definite times."

"I know, George, but that's after the kidnapping," Nancy said. "And Deputy Austin said that no kidnapping had taken place."

"Maybe they have to be at a certain place at a certain time in order to kidnap this person," Derek said. "Maybe that's the only time the person will be there."

"Yeah!" George agreed. "Maybe that person will only be by himself for a few minutes and that's when they'll do it."

"I've heard of that before," said Bess. "People are kidnapped when they get onto elevators or out of their cars to check their mailboxes."

Up ahead, Jimmy slowed down for a red light but then went through it.

When Derek got to the intersection, they had to wait for several cars, but then the light changed.

But Jimmy Boyd's pickup had already disappeared.

When they reached the next intersection, Nancy checked both directions. "Turn left," she said. She was sure she could make out the taillights of Jimmy's pickup.

Soon they entered a residential area of very large homes. There were very few cars on the street, and Nancy knew there was a good chance that Jimmy would spot them, so they followed very slowly.

Jimmy Boyd stopped his pickup in front of a large and expensive-looking house.

"Do you think he's going to kidnap whoever lives here?" Bess whispered. "Maybe we should warn them."

"I think we should call the police," George suggested.

Nancy hesitated. "Let's wait to see exactly what he and Mary have planned," she said. "The police weren't too interested in talking to me earlier. I want to make sure that something is actually happening before we get them involved."

The passenger side door opened, and Mary got out and ran up to the house.

"She's headed straight for the front door," Bess said. "That's weird. What's she going to do, ring the bell and then grab the person when he answers the door?"

But Mary didn't ring the bell. She just opened the front door and went inside.

"Wait here," Nancy said. "I'm going to see what Mary's up to."

Nancy ducked low, darting from tree to tree, until she reached the side of the house.

She just hoped that she'd be able to see what was going on through a window.

Luckily, she found a small window in a door at the back of the house that let her see through to what looked like a den. Nancy gasped. Mary Harvey was standing beside the girl that Derek had been talking to in the Student Union!

Nancy racked her brain, trying to remember the girl's name! Finally it came to her. Candace!

But what was Mary doing here? Nancy wondered. Did she and Jimmy plan to kidnap Candace? If they did, this was a strange way of going about it.

Besides, Mary and Candace seemed to be arguing about something. This wasn't the way kidnappings usually happened, Nancy knew. The kidnapper grabbed the victim. He didn't argue with him or her about whether they were going to be kidnapped.

Just then Candace whirled around, and Nancy saw she had a pout on her face. There was no sign of fear. Candace suddenly plopped down in a chair. She looked exasperated, not scared. Mary sat down next to her and began smoothing Candace's hair. Kidnappers didn't do that, either, Nancy knew.

Suddenly Nancy heard something behind her and turned. She hadn't realized that she was standing next to a gate that led to the backyard.

Nancy held her breath. There was someone behind it. She felt a chill go up her back to the base of her neck. Had Jimmy come through on the other side? Was he now waiting to grab her?

Nancy heard a low growl and realized that it was a dog!

Before she could decide what to do, the dog started barking loudly. Nancy glanced back through the window and saw that Mary and Candace were looking right at the window. She had to get out of there.

Nancy started running back to the street, ducking behind the trees so Jimmy Boyd wouldn't see her, but when she got to the last tree, at the edge of the yard, she stopped. Derek's car was gone!

She looked down the street. She could see Jimmy's pickup, but Derek's car was nowhere in sight.

Where did they go? Nancy wondered. Why did they leave?

Then it occurred to her that maybe Derek had gotten frightened and decided to hide the car. Nancy was sure that Derek wouldn't have driven past Jimmy's pickup, so that meant he must have backed up and parked around the corner.

Bess and George would have guessed that Nancy knew what happened, so they wouldn't have stopped Derek.

Nancy sprinted toward the end of the block, hoping that Jimmy Boyd wouldn't be looking out his rear window or that Candace and Mary hadn't come out to see who had disturbed the dog.

When Nancy reached the end of the block, she

checked both directions but didn't see Derek's car anywhere. "Where could they be?" Nancy wondered aloud.

Then it occurred to her that maybe Derek had gone to get the police.

What now? Nancy wondered.

She knew she didn't want to walk back down the street toward Candace's house, and that left only one option. She had to decide which way to go: right or left.

Nancy went right.

There were no sidewalks in this subdivision, so she had to walk in the street. Suddenly behind her she heard a noise that chilled her. It sounded exactly like Jimmy Boyd's pickup.

Nancy quickly decided to run up onto a lawn and hide, but just as she stepped up onto the curb, she was caught in the headlights of the pickup.

Nancy sprinted toward the nearest bush, but behind her she heard the pickup stop and then a door open. Over her shoulder she saw Jimmy Boyd leap from the pickup and race toward her.

11

Jimmy's Story

Nancy stumbled over a garden hose and went tumbling to the ground.

Suddenly a porch light went on.

"I've got you now!" Jimmy Boyd shouted from the middle of the lawn.

Just as suddenly the porch light went out.

No one wants to get involved, Nancy thought angrily. She scrambled up, but her feet got tangled in some of the low branches of the bush.

Jimmy Boyd was on her in a flash. He grabbed her arm. Nancy started kicking wildly. If she could only get on her feet, she thought, she could use her martial arts skills to escape.

"You're not going to get away with this!" Nancy

cried, trying to get out of Jimmy's hold, but his grip was like a vise.

She kicked at Jimmy's legs, landing a couple of blows, but still he held on tightly.

As Nancy struggled to break free, she saw that Jimmy hadn't shut the door of his pickup. The dome light was on, and she caught a glimpse of Mary.

Nancy decided that her best option was to talk to the girl, to make her realize that what she was doing could get her sent to prison for a long time.

When Nancy quit struggling, Jimmy slightly loosened his firm grip on her and led her to the passenger side of the pickup. Mary was now standing by the door, so Nancy would have to get in the middle.

"This is wrong, Mary," Nancy said. "You shouldn't have let Jimmy talk you into this."

"Get in, Nancy," Mary said angrily.

Nancy jerked her arm away from Jimmy, thinking that he might be taken by surprise and that she could escape, but Jimmy quickly clamped his strong fingers around her wrist.

"No, you don't," he said.

Nancy knew it was useless to try to get away from two of them, so she climbed up on to the running board and got in the middle.

Jimmy peeled out down the street before Mary had shut her door.

"Jimmy! Stop that!" Mary cried as she struggled to get the door closed.

To Nancy's surprise, Jimmy slowed down. "I'm sorry," he said. "I wasn't thinking."

This wasn't what Nancy expected to hear. Jimmy didn't sound like the angry man who had grabbed her just a few minutes earlier.

"Why were you spying on us, Nancy?" Mary suddenly asked.

The tone of her voice also surprised Nancy. She didn't seem angry, either. "I wasn't spying," Nancy said. "I was just trying to stop you from kidnapping Candace."

"What?" Jimmy cried.

"That's the craziest thing I've ever heard," Mary said. "Candace is my sister."

Nancy was stunned. "Your sister?"

"Yes," Mary replied. "Well, she's really my half-sister. We have the same mother, but her father is Dr. Johnson, the director of the tornado laboratory at the university."

"I don't understand," Nancy said.

"Quit playing games, Nancy!" said Jimmy. "Mary and I know what you people are really planning to do."

"What are you talking about?" Nancy asked. "What people?"

"The people with you at Bertha's farm," Jimmy said. "You're not going to get away with this!"

Nancy's head was beginning to spin. Nothing was making sense to her. "What is it that you think we're planning?" she asked.

When Jimmy didn't say anything, Nancy said, "You're the one who hit me over the head and stole that duffel bag, aren't you?"

Jimmy slammed on the brakes, throwing Nancy and Mary against their seat belts.

"What are you talking about?" he said. He gave Nancy a hard look. "Somebody took that duffel bag from you?"

Nancy returned his glare. "Yes, *somebody* did," she said.

Jimmy started back down the road. "Well, it wasn't me," he answered.

Nancy wasn't sure she believed him, but she wasn't going to say anything else about it. There was no point getting Jimmy angry again.

Just then a car sped past them. Jimmy's headlights illuminated the rear end before it disappeared into the darkness ahead of them.

That looks like Derek's car, Nancy thought. What was he doing out here? Then it occurred to her that he could be taking Bess and George back to the farm, which meant they must be headed in that direction, too. Was Jimmy Boyd taking her home?

Nancy looked at him. "I don't understand. You just kidnapped me. Why are you bringing me back to the farm?"

Jimmy Boyd shook his head. "You have some of the weirdest ideas," he said.

"Why in the world would we kidnap you?" Mary asked. Nancy thought she seemed genuinely surprised at the accusation.

Was Jimmy Boyd telling the truth about not taking the duffel bag? But if he didn't do it, who did? Nancy wondered.

Jimmy reached the turnoff to the farm and headed up the rutted lane.

Abruptly they were blinded by two bright lights.

"Jimmy!" Mary screamed. "That car's coming right toward us."

Jimmy jerked the steering wheel and swerved just in time to miss being hit.

That *is* Derek's car! Nancy realized. Why is he driving so crazily?

"What's wrong with that guy?" Mary said. "He's going to get someone killed."

Nancy was wondering the same thing. She certainly hoped that Derek had dropped off Bess and George. She had to know they were all right.

As Jimmy pulled up in front of the farmhouse, Bess and George came outside and stood on the porch. Even though the porch light was dim, Nancy could see that they were all right.

Suddenly Nancy had an idea. "I wish you'd both come inside," she said. "Hannah probably has something to drink, and we can talk about what's been happening."

Mary looked at Jimmy. "I think we should," she said. "I'm really confused about everything."

Nancy could see that Jimmy was thinking it over. Finally he said, "Okay."

As the three of them got out of the pickup, Bess and George hurried to greet Nancy.

"Are you all right?" Bess asked.

"I'm fine," Nancy replied. "What about you two?"

"We're okay, but we were so worried about you," George said. She eyed Jimmy and Mary suspiciously. "What are they doing here?" she whispered.

"I'll explain later," Nancy whispered back. "Come on inside," she said to Jimmy and Mary. "It'll be good to get this all out in the open."

Jimmy and Mary followed Nancy, Bess, and George into the house.

"Nancy!" Hannah cried. "I was worried sick about you."

"I'm fine," Nancy said.

Mr. Drew came into the room. "She wasn't the only one who was worried," he said. He looked at Jimmy and Mary. "I see we have guests."

"I asked Jimmy and Mary to come in for a few minutes," Nancy explained. "There are several things we need to talk about."

"Well, have a seat," Mr. Drew said. He motioned

to two comfortable side chairs next to the couch. "Hannah has just made some fresh lemonade."

Nancy grinned. "What did I tell you?"

"That sounds wonderful," Mary said.

Jimmy nodded. "Thank you," he added.

Rather than acting angry and gruff, Jimmy Boyd now seemed shy, not at all the way he had at their first encounter.

After Hannah had served everyone lemonade, Nancy asked Jimmy to tell them his story.

"Bertha promised me this farm," Jimmy began, "and I've got the letters to prove it." He hesitated. "Well, I did have them, until something happened to the duffel bag I put them in."

"Go on," Nancy said.

"Well, Bertha wrote me letters when I was in the army," Jimmy said. "She knew my mom before she died, so I guess she thought I was lonely. I was, so I started writing her back. It was just like hearing from my mother. In fact, I started to think of her as my mother, and when I got out of the army, I came back to Medicine Bluff and told her that.

"It kind of surprised her, because she really had just written to me as a friend, but she started doing more and more for me, and I started helping out more and more on the farm. Bertha even let me put some of my things in the barn, because I was staying in a trailer in town and didn't have room to store things. She knew I loved this place and told me in several letters that she was going to leave it to me."

"Those were the letters in the duffel bag?" Mr. Drew said.

Jimmy nodded. "The tornado must have blown them away when it destroyed the barn."

"A barn seems like a funny place to put important papers," Nancy said.

"I know," Jimmy said, "but I just loved being up in the loft."

"You did?" George asked.

Jimmy nodded. "I would lie in the hay and look up at the sky through the cracks in the roof. It relaxed me."

"He was always a different person when he came back from the farm," Mary said. "It just did something for him."

"What about the duffel bag *you* lost?" Nancy asked Mary. "What do you think happened to it?"

Mary blushed. "I didn't really lose one," she admitted. "I don't live in a mobile home that was lost, either. Sorry. Jimmy told me about the argument he had with you, and I thought if I told you the duffel bag was mine, you'd let me have it."

Nancy knew that if both Jimmy and Mary were telling the truth, she was back at the beginning in her attempt to solve the mystery.

Of course, some people were really good at making up stories that tugged at people's heartstrings, and both Jimmy and Mary had done a good job with Hannah.

"Have some more cookies and lemonade," Hannah gently said to them both.

"Sounds good to me," Jimmy answered.

Nancy turned sharply. She thought she had heard a car door slam, but no one else seemed to have noticed it.

While everyone else was busy getting refills of lemonade and cookies, Nancy went to the window. Two bright taillights were disappearing down the lane. Had someone been spying on them? she wondered.

12

Derek Has a Plan

"I'm sorry to have to break this to you, Jimmy," Nancy said, "but the duffel bag we found in the tree didn't have any letters to you from Bertha."

Jimmy looked stunned.

"It didn't, Jimmy," Mr. Drew added. "We would tell you if it did."

"Well, where did it come from, then, if it didn't come from the barn?" Jimmy asked.

That's what Nancy wanted to know. "I suppose it could have come from anywhere," she replied. "Someone at the tornado laboratory told me it could have come from as far as twenty miles away."

"Twenty miles!" Hannah said.

Nancy nodded. Of course, Derek thought that the tornado had picked the duffel bag up in the barn and blown it into the tree. And that would mean the duffel bag could be Jimmy's. But how did that explain the ransom notes? Something was not right here, Nancy knew.

Was Jimmy lying about what was in the duffel bag? Nancy had only Jimmy's word that Bertha had promised him the farm. He could just be making that up, she knew. Or maybe Derek's calculations were wrong.

"What *was* in the duffel bag?" Mary asked.

Bess and George looked at Nancy.

"That's something that the police don't want me to talk about," Nancy said. They really wouldn't, she told herself, if they had just taken her seriously. "And it's not really fair to involve you if a crime's about to be committed."

Nancy watched to see Jimmy and Mary's reaction, but they both seemed to accept Nancy's explanation. They were either good actors or they really didn't know about the ransom notes.

"We'd better go. It's getting late," Mary said. "I have to be at the bank early tomorrow."

"Thanks for bringing me home," Nancy said. "I'm sorry for all of the confusion."

"Oh, that's all right," Mary said. She leaned over to Nancy and whispered, "Jimmy is really upset about losing those letters. This farm was all he thought about when he was in the army. It kept him going. Please try to help him."

"I'll do what I can," Nancy whispered back.

Mary gave Nancy a friendly smile, then followed Jimmy out to the pickup.

Bess and George stood behind Nancy as she watched the taillights of Jimmy's pickup wink into the darkness.

"What do you think, Nancy?" Bess asked. "Were they telling the truth?"

"I don't know," Nancy replied. She turned and raised an eyebrow at both of them. "What I want to know now is why you drove off and left me?"

"We didn't," George protested. "You left us!"

Nancy gave them a questioning look. "What do you mean? I searched all over for you and couldn't find you anywhere."

"That's because we were too well hidden," George said.

"You'll have to explain that," Nancy said.

"Well, Derek started getting nervous," Bess said. "He was sure that any minute Jimmy would see us, so he decided to find someplace else to park."

"So he backed up, then pulled into a driveway and parked behind some bushes," George said.

"We saw you running away from the house," Bess said, "but by the time Derek got his car started, you had disappeared."

Something about the expression on Bess's face made Nancy ask, "What's wrong?"

"Well, maybe I shouldn't say this, Nancy, because I know you like Derek," Bess said, "but, well, there was something about what Derek did that made me think he was trying to hide from you."

"Where did you get that notion, Bess?" George asked. "Derek was really upset that we couldn't find Nancy after he got the car started."

Nancy was getting tired, so she decided not to pursue the matter now, but it was something to think about because Bess had always been a pretty good judge of character.

The next morning Nancy was up early. When she went into the kitchen, Hannah had already made breakfast for Mr. Drew. He was sitting alone at the table, reading some legal briefs.

"Well, good morning," Mr. Drew said. "I thought you might sleep late after such an exciting evening."

"No, I feel fine," Nancy said. "It must be all this country air."

"I was thinking the same thing," Mr. Drew said. "Sit down and have some breakfast with me. We haven't had a chance to talk since we got here."

Nancy pulled out a chair, then buttered a piece of toast and poured herself a glass of orange juice.

"Will you be needing Bertha's car today?" Nancy asked.

Mr. Drew thought for a minute. "No. We've taken care of most of the necessary legal matters. Hannah wants to finish looking through some of Bertha's things. And I was going to catch up on some work. Why?"

"I need to go into Medicine Bluff. I thought Bess and George could go with me. I have to tie up some loose ends," Nancy said. "Since last night, I don't know what to believe. Actually, I don't know *whom* to believe."

Mr. Drew put down the papers he had been reading. "Nancy, I've been thinking about something," he said. "Maybe those ransom notes were just a prank after all."

"I've thought about that, Dad," Nancy told him, "but I have a feeling that they weren't."

Just then Bess and George came into the kitchen.

"There's something about breakfast on a farm that makes me ravenous," Bess said.

Nancy laughed. "Bess! Get real! There's just something about *food* that makes you ravenous."

George and Bess sat down and began filling their plates. Hannah put more toast and jam and orange juice on the table. "Bacon and eggs anyone?"

"Sounds good to me," George said.

"Me, too," Bess agreed.

Nancy sighed. "So much for getting an early start," she said.

"What's up?" George asked.

"I need to talk to Derek," Nancy said. "Jimmy and Mary brought up some things I hadn't thought about."

"I know what you mean," Bess said. "They don't seem as bad as I thought they were."

Nancy realized that Bess had just said what she had been thinking but didn't really want to admit.

"Well, I don't have to have eggs," Bess said.

"Me, either," George said. "Just let me finish my toast and orange juice."

"I don't mean to rush you," Nancy protested.

George finished off her orange juice. "No, no!" she said with a grin. "I don't want to keep the great Nancy Drew waiting. We can't let eggs and bacon get in the way of a mystery to be solved!"

Nancy rolled her eyes.

True to their word, after just a few minutes, Bess and George were ready to leave for Medicine Bluff.

"Get ready for the roller coaster ride," Nancy said, as she began maneuvering over the ruts in the lane that led to the road. Even with Nancy's driving skill, the car still bounced up and down violently.

"This thing needs some shocks badly," George said. "It's going to shake my breakfast up."

"That is so gross, George!" Bess said.

Finally they reached the end of the lane, and Nancy turned left to head into Medicine Bluff.

"Oh, no!" Bess gasped.

"What's wrong?" Nancy asked.

"Don't look now," Bess said, "but I think Jimmy Boyd's pickup is behind us!"

Nancy glanced in the rearview mirror and saw that Bess was right. "Where'd he come from?" she asked calmly.

George turned to look out the rear window. "He must have been parked in that grove of trees back there," she said. "He was probably waiting for us."

"Why would he do that?" Bess asked.

Nancy thought she knew. "Maybe he plans to kidnap all three of us," she said.

"Nancy!" Bess gasped. "That's not funny!"

"I'm not joking," Nancy said as she increased her speed. "Last night I thought perhaps he and Mary were telling the truth. Now I'm not so sure."

"He's gaining on us, Nancy," George said.

"Is he going to try to ram us?" Bess asked, panic in her voice.

"I hope not," Nancy said. She wasn't sure that Bertha's car was up to the chase.

Nancy increased her speed as much as she dared on the narrow country road. Jimmy stayed right behind her.

"How could we have been so dumb?" Bess cried.

"What do you mean?" George asked.

"Why would we even think they were telling the truth?" Bess said.

"I'm sure it was all planned," Nancy said, angry at herself for falling into Jimmy Boyd's trap. "They probably wanted us to feel sorry for them, so we'd be off our guard."

"Well, it certainly worked," George said.

Bess screamed as Nancy took a sharp curve and the right tires hit the edge of a ditch, but Nancy expertly maneuvered the old car back onto the road and increased her speed.

"I see the outskirts of Medicine Bluff," George said.

Nancy took a deep breath. They weren't safe yet, she knew, but at least now the road wasn't as narrow.

Nancy floored the accelerator, and the old car shot forward, sending the three of them against their seats.

"Yikes!" Bess said. "I feel like I'm in an airplane."

"I wish we could take off," George said. "That would be a way to get away from Jimmy Boyd."

Nancy glanced in the rearview mirror and realized that they were leaving Jimmy farther and farther behind, but she didn't take her foot off the accelerator until they reached the Medicine

Bluff city limits. Then she braked to the speed limit.

"We beat him," Bess said.

"I'm not sure we did," Nancy said.

"What do you mean?" George asked.

"I think he had started slowing down before I made the final push," Nancy said. "Maybe he was just trying to scare us."

"Well, he certainly scared me," Bess said.

"Why would he want to do that?" George asked. "I'm sure that after last night he thought we believed them."

"Well, maybe this morning, he thought we hadn't," Nancy said. "I don't know. It's all so weird."

They had reached the edge of downtown Medicine Bluff, and Nancy headed toward the university.

"Where are we meeting Derek?" Bess asked.

"He said he's usually at the Student Union, so I thought we'd go there first," Nancy said.

"Doesn't he have a home?" George asked.

"Of course he does, but he probably doesn't want us to see it," Nancy said. "Some people feel that way about where they live."

They found Derek in the food court, eating a breakfast taco, and joined him at his table.

"That looks good," Bess said. She began scanning the menus of the various restaurant.

"Bess!" Nancy said. "Did you forget something?"

Bess gave her a puzzled look. "What?"

George laughed. "We've already had breakfast!"

"Oh, yeah. Right," Bess said, a blush spreading across her face. She gave Derek's breakfast taco another glance. "Too bad."

Derek wiped his mouth with a paper napkin. "I'm sorry about last night, Nancy. Sometimes that dumb car of mine just won't start."

"Don't worry about it," Nancy said. "I got home all right."

Nancy hadn't planned to tell Derek anything, but Jimmy Boyd's behavior this morning made her decide to take him into her confidence. She recounted everything that had happened since she had left Derek, Bess, and George.

"We even believed them," Bess added.

"Until Jimmy Boyd chased us into town this morning," George said.

"You're making them nervous, Nancy," Derek said. "So you need to be careful. I think Jimmy Boyd is dangerous."

"I can handle him," Nancy said.

"It's not just you, Nancy," Derek said. "He and Mary may try to get rid of your entire family."

Bess and George gasped.

Derek could be right, Nancy thought, and wondered if it was safe for her father and Hannah to be alone in the farmhouse.

"But that doesn't really make sense, Derek," Nancy said. "Even if Jimmy did something to all of us, that wouldn't mean he'd get the farm."

"It might, Nancy," Derek insisted. "What if he really does have a letter from Bertha? If Hannah is no longer in the picture, some judge just might decide to give it to him."

"Derek could be right," Bess said.

"Do you know whose house we were at last night?" Nancy asked Derek.

Derek hesitated. "Whose?" he finally said.

"Candace Johnson's," Nancy said. "She's Dr. Johnson's daughter."

Derek blinked. "Really?" He shrugged. "Well, there goes that relationship." He looked over at Bess. "I don't think I can eat this other taco. Do you want it?"

"Are you sure?" Bess said.

Derek nodded.

Bess picked up the breakfast taco from Derek's plate. "Well, I certainly wouldn't want it to go to waste," she said.

Nancy kept looking at Derek. She was surprised that he had dismissed the information about Candace Johnson so quickly.

Derek crinkled his eyes. "Why are you staring at me?" he asked. "Do I have crumbs on my mouth?" He grinned at her.

"No, no," Nancy said hurriedly. "I was just wondering what we should do now."

"Well, I just thought of a way to trap Jimmy and Mary," Derek said.

"Let's hear it," Nancy said.

"What are your plans for the next few days?" Derek asked.

"We really haven't talked about doing anything except packing to go home," Nancy said. "Dad's getting the RV out of the shop later today."

"Then tell your dad that you want to drive to Lawton tomorrow," Derek said. "Tell him you want to see Fort Sill and the Wichita Mountains."

"How is that going to trap Jimmy and Mary?" Nancy asked.

"Call Jimmy up to say goodbye. Tell him you're leaving. Wish him luck. Whatever," Derek said. "If he thinks you're gone, he and Mary might go ahead with their kidnapping plans."

"Hmm, Derek, that might work," Nancy said, ignoring the strange looks that Bess and George were giving her. "We only have a couple more days in Medicine Bluff, and I can't leave thinking that I had information that would stop a kidnapping from taking place and didn't act on it." She turned to Bess and George. "You'll have to help me convince Dad to let me stay behind while you guys go to Lawton."

"Can't we stay with you, Nancy?" Bess pleaded.

"Yeah, Nancy, we'll miss all of the fun," George said.

"Sorry, girls," Derek said. "I think it would be better if Nancy were by herself. I can meet you at the Student Union."

"Derek's right. Jimmy and Mary need to believe that we're all leaving," Nancy said. "If they do, we may be able to trap them—even if I have to act as bait."

13

Trapped!

All afternoon Nancy, Bess, and George practiced how they'd present Derek's plan to Mr. Drew.

Finally Nancy just decided to come right out and tell him that she thought it was her only chance to catch the kidnappers before they left for River Heights.

"Well, I'm not happy about this, but I trust your instincts," Carson Drew finally said. "You usually know what you're doing."

"Thanks, Dad. I knew you'd understand," Nancy said. "I have to do all I can to stop this kidnapping."

After calling Jimmy to tell him they were leaving the next day, Nancy tried to play a card game with

Bess, George, and Hannah but was unable to concentrate. They finally decided to play something that didn't include her, and Nancy was glad because she wanted to think about the plan for the next day.

Nancy was up after everyone else had gone to bed. Once the house was totally quiet, Nancy sat on the front porch. There was a pleasant breeze that cooled her face and ruffled her hair. It was wonderfully peaceful out in the country, she decided, although she didn't know if she could ever live too far from River Heights.

Finally several pesky mosquitoes forced her inside, where Bess and George were already sound asleep. Nancy wanted to discuss some of her options with them, and she thought about waking them but decided that wouldn't be fair. She had had her chance for discussion, so she willed herself to relax and in a few minutes started feeling pleasantly drowsy. Right before she fell asleep, she thought she heard footsteps on the front porch.

When Nancy finally awakened the next morning, everyone else was dressed and ready to go, so she had only a couple of minutes to grab a piece of toast and a small glass of orange juice before Mr. Drew pulled the RV in front of the house.

"What are those suitcases for?" Nancy asked

when she saw Bess and George heading out the door, each carrying one.

"Remember? We're supposed to be going home?" George said. "But don't worry, Hannah has already carried out two empty suitcases for you. If Jimmy Boyd is watching, it will look as though we're leaving town."

"Great idea!" Nancy said. "I hadn't thought of that."

Nancy made a great show of locking the front door and looking around, pretending to check to make sure that things were secure before she got into the RV.

"If he breaks into the farmhouse, he'll know we haven't left," George said. "All our things are still there."

"I don't think he'll do that," Nancy said. "If he's watching the house, the suitcases should convince him that we're gone."

"I just hope this works out the way you have it planned, Nancy," Mr. Drew said.

"So do I, Dad," Nancy said. "So do I."

Mr. Drew maneuvered the RV as carefully as he could over the rutted driveway, but the huge vehicle still bounced up and down, causing the suitcases to slide around on the floor.

Finally they reached the highway and turned toward Medicine Bluff.

"There he is!" Nancy said. "You can barely see it, but that's Jimmy Boyd's pickup."

Just like the day before, Jimmy's pickup was half-hidden in a clump of trees down the road. If Nancy hadn't been looking for it, she probably wouldn't have noticed it.

"Here's he comes!" Bess cried. "He's going to follow us into town."

"Do you think he'll try to kidnap all of us today?" Bess said.

"What?" Hannah cried. "What are you talking about?"

Nancy explained what had happened the day before when she and Bess and George drove into Medicine Bluff.

"Do you still want to go through with this, Nancy?" Carson Drew said. "It looks as if Jimmy is getting desperate."

"I think he was just trying to scare us, Dad," Nancy hurriedly explained. She turned to look out the rear window. Jimmy Boyd was staying some distance behind. Nancy knew she was right. Jimmy Boyd was just going to follow them until he was satisfied that they were leaving Medicine Bluff.

Nancy had already worked it out with her father how she was going to give Jimmy the slip.

"That's the convenience store up there, Dad," Nancy said. "That's where we'll stop for gas."

"Is this where you leave us?" George asked.

Nancy nodded. "If Jimmy does what I think he'll do, it'll be easy."

"What do you think he'll do?" Bess asked as Mr. Drew pulled the RV up to one of the self-serve pumps.

Nancy was following Jimmy's movements out the side window of the RV. "Just what he's doing now," she said. "He's not stopping. He's going to circle the block. When he's out of sight, I'll slip out of the RV and hide in the women's rest room."

"He's turned the corner, Nancy!" George cried.

Mr. Drew got out and started filling up the RV.

"This is it, then," Nancy said. "Have fun. When you get back, let's hope that Jimmy and Mary will be in jail."

"Be careful, Nancy," Hannah pleaded.

Nancy squeezed Hannah's hand. "Don't worry. I'll be just fine." With a wave to Bess and George, she slipped out of the RV. She used the street-side door so no one in the convenience store would see her getting out.

"I'll see you soon, Nancy," Carson Drew whispered when Nancy passed by the gasoline pump.

"Right, Dad," Nancy whispered back without looking at him. She didn't want anyone connecting the two of them to the RV and wondering why Nancy didn't get back into it when it pulled out.

Inside the convenience store Nancy quickly found the women's rest room. She was glad that it was empty and that it was sparkling clean. She wouldn't mind staying in here for several minutes until she felt that Jimmy Boyd was back on the road, following the RV.

By her watch, Nancy waited for fifteen minutes. A couple of times people knocked on the door, but Nancy refused to be hurried.

Finally she opened the door of the rest room and was confronted by a lady who gave her a dirty look. "Sorry," Nancy said pleasantly.

Nancy was glad that the clerk was waiting on another customer and didn't pay any attention to her. She slowly wandered down the aisles of the store, pretending to shop as she made her way toward the front, where she could look out the windows to see if the RV was gone.

It was.

Nancy positioned herself by the magazine rack, picked up a couple of the magazines and pretended to leaf through them but really looked at the street to make sure that Jimmy Boyd had also driven by and seen that the RV was gone.

Finally, when Nancy felt the eyes of the clerk on her, she sighed, acting as though she simply couldn't find what she wanted, and left the store.

She turned sharply to the left, wanting to get out of the clerk's line of vision as soon as possible, and headed in the direction of downtown. She walked a block over, so she wouldn't be on the main street but parallel to it until she reached the street that led to the university.

It was a pleasant morning for walking, and any other time Nancy Drew would have enjoyed window-shopping, especially in the antique stores that lined this street. There were all kinds of interesting things that had historical significance for Medicine Bluff. She found several items that would look great in their house in River Heights, but there was no time for shopping today. She had things that had to be taken care of.

When Nancy reached University Avenue, she turned in the direction of the campus but had only gone a block when she heard someone honk.

Her heart skipped a beat. Had Jimmy Boyd spotted her? she wondered. But when she turned around, Derek was pulling up to the curb.

"Get in," he called to her.

Nancy opened the passenger side door, but Derek's backpack was piled on the seat.

"Oh, sorry about that," Derek said. "Just toss it in the back."

Nancy picked up the backpack, but it was too heavy just to toss over the seat, so she pulled it out and opened the back door. Just as she dropped the backpack onto the backseat, she saw something that looked very familiar. She glanced up at Derek. He was busy tuning the radio. I'll check it out later, she decided.

"I see the plan worked," Derek said as Nancy fastened her seat belt.

"Like a charm," Nancy said. "No problem at all." She looked at him. "But what are you doing here?" she asked. "I thought we were supposed to meet at the Student Union."

"I got restless. I thought I'd probably find you along here," Derek said as he pulled away from the curb and headed back toward Main Street. "So everyone's gone to Lawton? You're the only one in Medicine Bluff?"

Nancy nodded. "I'm the only one," she said. She smiled at Derek.

Derek smiled back but didn't say anything.

"I think the first thing we should do is stake out Mary's house," Nancy said. "I'm sure that Jimmy will follow the RV only until he's sure we've left town and aren't coming back. Then he'll return to Medicine Bluff. In fact, he may already be back."

"Could be," Derek said. He was craning his neck to look through the front windshield. "Look at those clouds. Have you ever seen anything so beautiful in your life?"

Nancy looked to where Derek was pointing. To the west, there was a huge bank of black clouds on the horizon. "They look kind of scary to me," she said.

Derek turned to her. "They're heading this way,

too. Medicine Bluff is going to have a monster tornado before the day is over."

"Then we should work fast, don't you think?" Nancy said.

Derek took a deep breath, let it out, and then seemed to sink back into the seat of his car.

"I know how weather affects you, Derek," Nancy said, "but we've got to stay focused on the kidnapping."

Derek looked at his watch. "We need to go to my house first. I have some things I need to pick up."

"What kinds of things?" Nancy asked.

"Just storm chaser stuff," Derek said. "I'm not going to miss chasing what I know will be one of the biggest storms of the year."

"Okay, Derek, just stop the car," Nancy said. "I want out."

Derek continued to drive. In fact, Nancy was sure that he had even speeded up some.

"I mean it, Derek," Nancy said.

"Don't be angry, Nancy," Derek said. He was looking straight ahead. "A person has to do what he has to do."

"I know," Nancy said. "I have to solve this mystery." She nodded in the direction of the clouds. "That storm isn't even close to us."

"You're wrong, Nancy," Derek said. "It's moving fast."

Nancy looked again. Derek was right. The clouds

were much larger now than when Derek had first pointed them out to her. It was incredible how fast they had exploded.

"Well, after you get your equipment, could we just drive by Mary's house?" Nancy asked. "If Jimmy's pickup isn't there, then I won't say another word."

"Okay," Derek said.

They drove in silence for several minutes until they came to a stop outside a small frame house.

"You'll have to stay in the car," Derek said. "Mom doesn't like company."

"That's okay," Nancy said.

Derek pulled into the narrow driveway and stopped the car. "I won't be long," he said. He got out without glancing back at her. Nancy waited until Derek was inside the house, then she stood on her knees and looked over into the floorboard of the backseat.

"I was right!" she cried. "It *is* a green duffel bag!" Now everything was really beginning to fall into place.

Nancy thought she had glimpsed it when she had put Derek's backpack on the backseat, but she had to be positive.

If she could just reach the duffel bag and open it, she'd know for sure that it was Derek who was planning the kidnapping, not Jimmy Boyd or Mary Harvey. But the strap of the duffel bag was caught on something under the seat, so Nancy had to lean over even farther to get it.

She had just started to unzip it, when she heard the passenger door open. She wasn't able to straighten up before she felt a blow to her head and everything went dark.

14

F5

When Nancy opened her eyes, it felt as if she were rubbing sandpaper across them. Her head was pounding, but she could still make out the roar of an automobile as it raced down the highway. But what was that *thump-thump* she kept hearing?

She closed her eyes again. What had happened to her? She remembered driving with Derek to his house, but staying in the car, because he didn't want her to come inside. He had said something about his mother not liking company. That was it. Slowly it was all coming back.

Nancy opened her eyes again and looked over at Derek. For some reason, it seemed dark inside the car. Derek's face had a green cast to it, because of the light from the dashboard.

But why was it dark? Nancy wondered. Had she been unconscious that long?

Then a streak of lightning hit the road in front of them, causing Derek to swerve the automobile.

Nancy grabbed the armrest. A clap of thunder shook the car, literally causing it to vibrate. Suddenly Nancy realized that they were in the middle of a terrible thunderstorm and the *thump-thump* she had heard was the windshield wipers furiously trying to clear the sheets of rain.

"This is the really big one, Nancy," Derek said.

Nancy touched the back of her head. "What?" she groaned.

"This storm. It could be the worst one in history," Derek said. "According to the radio, the highway patrol has already spotted ten tornadoes on the ground." Derek laughed gleefully. "They're dancing all around Medicine Bluff. When they finally collide, there's going to be some party!"

He's mad! Nancy thought. He's totally out of his mind.

"Derek, please slow down," Nancy said, and fastened her seat belt. "You're going too fast in this rain."

"Oh, you can't go too fast, Nancy, when you want to catch up with a tornado," Derek said. He looked over at her. "And that's what we're doing."

Nancy was trying to think fast, but her head was

in no condition to deal with what she was hearing. All she wanted to do was close her eyes and go back to sleep, but she knew her life depended on staying awake.

Nancy tried to see through the sheets of rain that were lashing the car. "How do you even know where the tornadoes are?" she said. "You can't see anything."

"Oh, that's what makes me different, Nancy," Derek said. "I can *feel* where they are."

Nancy thought if she could keep him talking, she might give herself enough time to think of a way out of this mess. "What do you mean?" she asked.

"It has to do with atmospheric pressure," Derek explained. "I can feel the changes. I know how it feels when a tornado is around."

"You mean you know there are tornadoes around by the way you feel?" Nancy continued to question.

Derek grinned. "Yes! Yes!" For a minute he took his hands off the steering wheel and placed one on each ear. "My head's killing me, Nancy! It's the atmospheric pressure!"

The automobile hit the muddy shoulder and started to spin, but Derek grabbed the wheel and to Nancy's amazement expertly got it back onto the pavement.

"Derek, please don't do that again," Nancy pleaded. When Derek didn't say anything, she added, "Why don't we stop for a minute, just to see if we can actually see the tornadoes. It's such a blur outside the window."

Derek looked over at her. "You just want to stop so you can escape, don't you?"

Nancy looked into his eyes. She suddenly realized that they hadn't even talked about why Derek had hit her. Nothing had been said about the green duffel bag, either. "What are you talking about, Derek?" she said. "Why would I want to escape?"

For just a minute Nancy saw puzzlement in Derek's eyes and she thought maybe she could convince him that she hadn't seen anything, but then Derek said, "That green duffel bag is mine, Nancy. I'm the one planning the kidnapping."

"But you haven't done anything yet, Derek," Nancy told him. "If you never do it, then there's nothing the police can do to you, because they already think those ransom notes are a prank."

Derek was shaking his head. "It's too late, Nancy," he said. "I can't stop now. Everything is in motion. I've kidnapped you."

"No, you haven't," Nancy said. "I went with you willingly."

"But I'm not going to let you go," Derek said.

"Why not?" Nancy asked. "What are you planning to do?"

Derek laughed. "I'm not planning to do anything," he said, "but the tornado is." He pressed down on the accelerator, and the car shot forward into the heavy rain. "I have the perfect plan." He turned to her. "I had another perfect plan, too, until you interfered."

"I want to help you, Derek," Nancy said. "If you really want to go back to the university and study weather, there are ways."

"People will think that we both died," Derek continued, oblivious to what Nancy had just said, "but you'll be the only one who actually dies."

Nancy could feel herself getting frantic, but she willed herself to be calm. It would do no good to lose her composure now, she knew. She had to keep her wits about her. Even though everything was beginning to look hopeless, there had to be a way out of this. There just had to be.

"How can you make sure that happens, Derek?" Nancy said. She decided to get bold. "What if I survive and tell everyone what you tried to do?"

"Oh, you won't survive this tornado," Derek said. "The one we're heading toward is an F5." He grinned. "That means it has winds of over two hundred sixty-one miles per hour."

Nancy felt helpless. They were headed straight toward the worst possible tornado. She had seen pictures of what even weaker tornadoes could do to cars. They looked like tin cans that people had stepped on.

"You'll be killed, too, Derek," Nancy said. "What good will that do?"

"I haven't finished telling you my plan," Derek said. He sounded almost peevish.

Nancy didn't say anything, so Derek continued. "When the tornado is almost upon us, I'm going to knock you unconscious again, then I'm going to run for cover. People will just think that we were both killed while we were out chasing tornadoes. Something like that is bound to happen sooner or later, and people will just say it served us right for doing something so dumb. They'll find your body, but they'll just think that the tornado picked me up and carried me away. When they never find my body, it'll be like the start of a legend. People will think that a tornado that powerful might have carried me for a hundred miles. They might even think it dumped my body in a lake or a river."

"Derek, that's sick!" Nancy cried. "How can you do something like that to your mother?"

"Don't talk about my mother!" Derek screamed. "I'll tell her later what happened. I won't let her worry about me."

Now the car was going even faster, and Nancy could tell that they were in more severe weather, because the winds were buffeting the car, making it hard for Derek to steer. Nancy consciously tightened her seat belt. She noticed that Derek didn't have his buckled.

"When I get back to Medicine Bluff, I'm going to kidnap Candace Johnson and hold her for ransom,"

Derek continued, "but I'm only going to ask Dr. Johnson for enough money to buy a good storm-chasing vehicle. When I get it, I'm going to another part of the state, where they don't know me." He paused and looked over at Nancy. "I might even go up to Kansas. They have a lot of good tornadoes there, too."

Outside, the wind seemed to be screaming. The car was rocking so much that Nancy wondered how Derek could keep it on the road.

"You'll never get away with it, Derek!" She had to shout to make herself heard.

"Oh, yes, I will, Nancy," Derek said. "No one will suspect me, because I'll be dead."

"Candace Johnson will suspect you!" Nancy shouted at him. "She'll know you did it!"

"I'm not stupid, Nancy. I have that all planned. Candace won't be alive to tell anyone," Derek said. "After Dr. Johnson gives me the money, I'll tell him that he can find Candace in Big Bear Canyon. But by the time he gets there, Candace will have fallen, probably trying to escape." He looked at Nancy with vacant eyes. "That's a very dangerous place to go hiking, you know."

Nancy shuddered at the thought of what awaited Candace.

For several minutes Derek was silent, then he said, "My VORTEX vehicle will have the latest instruments to measure everything about a tornado.

It'll be even better than the new vehicles that the university just got."

For one of the few times in her life, Nancy felt like screaming out of pure frustration. She was in a car with a crazy person, traveling at an incredibly high rate of speed, through a terrible wind and rain storm, headed directly toward a monster tornado.

Then suddenly they were in it.

Derek's car was picked up by the tornado and was whirling around so fast that Nancy couldn't tell which was up and which was down. It was like nothing she had ever felt before.

Without his seatbelt to hold him, Derek was being tumbled all over the inside of the car.

Nancy was sure she could feel the car climbing higher into the tornado. This is it, she thought. This is the end.

15

Leaving Tornado Alley

All of a sudden Nancy thought she was in a movie dream sequence. Everything around her was moving in slow motion. She slowly turned her head and saw Derek sprawled in the backseat. Nancy was sure he was unconscious.

Then, just as suddenly as it had begun, everything returned to normal speed, and Nancy was being jerked in every direction, as the tornado tossed Derek's car around and around inside its funnel. Suddenly her seat belt ripped from one of its anchors, and now Nancy was being hurled around inside the car. She crashed into the dashboard. She crashed into the ceiling. She crashed into the steering wheel.

Frantically Nancy grabbed at the steering wheel

and hung on for dear life, but the movement of the car still flung her body against the doors.

Nancy also knew that she had to escape Derek's car or risk almost certain death when the tornado tired of tossing it around and flung it to the earth.

Nancy's leg brushed against the door handle on the driver's side, giving her an idea. She had absolutely no idea how far up she was inside the tornado's vortex, but if she could open the door, then drop through it, she might be able to land on something that wouldn't injure her. She remembered seeing fields and fields of wheat when she and Derek had driven around this area before, but she didn't know if she were in the same area.

Of course, she knew that she could also be injured by debris whirling inside the tornado or be carried miles away, but she decided to risk that.

A sudden violent motion flipped the car and tossed Nancy's body to the other side, but she held on to the steering wheel and gradually maneuvered her way back to where she could reach the door handle.

She gripped it and began to pull. She thought she felt it giving slightly, but nothing was happening. Then the car flipped again and Nancy lost her grip on the steering wheel. She was tossed from one side of the car to the other. Each time she hit the ceiling or the dashboard or one of the doors, she saw stars,

and she realized that she could be knocked unconscious.

But just as she hit one of the doors again, she
grabbed one of the handles and pulled with all of
her might.

The door popped open, and Nancy fell through
the opening.

For several seconds she simply floated in the air,
but then, just as suddenly, she was falling to the earth.

Nancy landed with a thud, which momentarily
took away her breath. Underneath her she could
feel a thick cushion of grass.

Nancy looked up and could see Derek's car still
being tossed around above her. It looked like a toy.
Nancy realized that she was still inside the funnel,
so she flipped herself and covered her head and
buried her face in the wet grass, hoping the tornado
wouldn't pick her up again.

Finally the wind stopped whirling around her, but
Nancy could still hear the roar of the tornado, like
the screaming of a thousand jet airplanes, so she
stayed where she was until her brain was finally able
to convince the rest of her body that the tornado
was moving away from her and that she was no
longer inside it.

Slowly Nancy raised her head and looked around.
She was in a grassy ditch next to the highway. Nancy
shuddered and realized that she was cold.

Turning, she could still see the tornado in the distance, perfectly shaped, as if it had been drawn on the sky. But her mind simply wouldn't allow her to believe that just a few minutes earlier, she had been inside that monster wind.

Suddenly Nancy blinked. In the distance a tiny car was falling to the ground—Derek's car. It was as if the tornado had spit it out.

Bracing herself with her hands, Nancy slowly tried to stand. Her legs were so weak that for a minute she didn't think they would support her.

She took a minute to examine herself. She was cut and bleeding and covered with mud, but she didn't seem to have any broken bones.

Then she heard another noise, one that had become so familiar to her in the few days that she had been in Medicine Bluff. It was Jimmy Boyd's pickup. She looked down the road and saw it coming.

The pickup screeched to a halt on the shoulder just above where she was standing.

Jimmy Boyd bounded out, and behind him came Bess and George. Nancy had never in her life seen such a welcome sight.

"Nancy! You're alive!" they cried.

When Bess and George reached her, she let them wrap their arms around her and tried not to wince when they squeezed too hard.

"What are you two doing with Jimmy?" she asked.

"It's a long story, but it's a good story," Bess said. "We'll tell you on the way to the hospital."

"Are Dad and Hannah all right?" Nancy asked.

"They're fine. They're on their way back to the farm," said George. "You're the one we were all worried about."

Nancy's legs were wobbly, so Jimmy picked her up and carried her to the pickup. He set her down gently, then Bess and George got in beside her. It was a tight squeeze, but they all made it.

"Now it's to the hospital to get you checked out," Jimmy said as he put the pickup in gear and headed into Medicine Bluff.

"I want to tell you what happened," Nancy said.

"You don't need to talk now," George said. "You just need to rest."

"George is right, Nancy. I can't believe you're still alive," Bess said. "I don't know what I would have done if you had been—"

"Well, she's all right, and that's the important thing," Jimmy said. "If she feels like talking, then let her talk, because people with concussions shouldn't be allowed to sleep."

"That's right," George said. "If you don't stay alert you might slip into a coma."

"Nancy!" Bess cried. "Start talking!"

Nancy smiled up at them. "I think I'm going to be all right. I really didn't have a hard landing at all."

Then she told them everything that had happened from the time she met Derek on her way to the university until they found her in the ditch beside the road. "I think Derek was in his car when it fell to the ground," Nancy finished. "I don't think he could still be alive."

"I'll tell the police about it as soon as we get to the hospital," Jimmy said. He shook his head. "I've never heard anything like this before. You are so lucky."

"I know that," Nancy said.

"So it was Derek all the time," George said. "He was going to kidnap Candace Johnson."

Nancy nodded. "When he suggested that crazy plan to get us out of town, I was sure it was him."

Bess gasped. "You were? And you still went through with your plan?"

"It was the only way I could catch him. It worked, too," Nancy said. "When I got into his car, I saw the green duffel bag on the floor. But he hit me over the head before I could do anything about it."

"How did he know you had it in the first place?" George asked. "You hadn't even met him then."

"That's my fault," Jimmy said.

Nancy looked at him. "Your fault?"

"Yes, I mentioned it to him when he came by to ask me about dating Candace Johnson," Jimmy said. "I told him that I thought you and your family were trying to steal the farm from me."

"Did he know where you kept your things in the barn?" Nancy asked.

Jimmy nodded. "He'd come by from time to time, when I was there, to try to get me to get him a date with Candace. He knew that Candace liked me because I was dating her half-sister."

"I'm sure he was hoping to frame you for the kidnapping," Nancy said. "He must have removed Bertha's letters from the duffel bag and put the ransom notes in it instead. He was probably going to call the police after the kidnapping and give them an 'anonymous' tip on where to find it. But then the tornado blew the duffel bag into the tree before he could carry out his plan." Nancy yawned. "Now tell me how the three of you got together," she said.

Jimmy looked over at her and grinned. "Your trick worked, Nancy. I followed the RV out of town, and it's a good thing, too, because it had two flats just a few miles from Medicine Bluff."

"Really?" Nancy said.

George nodded. "It sounded like a big explosion," she said.

"Jimmy stopped to help," Bess said.

"Why?" Nancy asked.

"I had already decided I was wrong about you and your family," Jimmy said, "but I was following you just to make sure you were leaving, because I wanted to search the farmhouse for those letters."

"You mean they really exist?" Nancy said.

"Yes, they exist," Jimmy said. "I thought maybe you had found them and had hidden them because you didn't want me to have the farm."

"We never had them," Nancy said. "If we had found them, we wouldn't have done something like that."

"I was afraid of that," Jimmy said. He sighed. "Now I don't know what to do."

"Don't worry about it, Jimmy," Nancy said. She yawned and closed her eyes. "Dad will figure something out."

"Nancy!" Bess cried. "Open your eyes!"

Nancy opened her eyes. "Sorry. It's just that I'm getting so sleepy."

"How much farther to the hospital?" George asked Jimmy.

"Just a couple of miles," Jimmy replied. He pushed the accelerator harder and the pickup shot forward.

"I still don't understand how you knew where to find me," Nancy said.

"It wasn't hard. When Bess and George told me the whole story, I put two and two together," Jimmy explained, "and I realized that it was Derek who was planning the kidnapping. But I also knew he would never miss a monster storm."

"Here's the hospital," Bess said.

Jimmy screeched to a halt in front of the emergency entrance and began honking his horn. In just a few seconds two attendants were rushing Nancy into the emergency room.

Later that night Nancy was back at the farm-house, the doctors having pronounced her okay. She was suffering from mild exhaustion, but they had re-leased her when she promised to get plenty of bed rest.

Before she went to bed, though, Nancy called the Medicine Bluff Police Department. They told her that Derek had not survived the tornado. Then Nancy decided to telephone Derek's mother. She had a question she wanted to ask her.

True to her word, Nancy was still in bed the next morning, with several pillows behind her back, eat-ing the light breakfast that Hannah had prepared especially for her.

Nancy was surrounded by Jimmy and Mary and Bess and George and Mr. Drew. Hannah bustled in from time to time to fluff Nancy's pillows and to see if she needed any more eggs.

"No, no, Hannah, I've had enough," Nancy pleaded. "Anyway, I need to get up and get packed if we're going to leave this morning."

"Everything's packed, young lady," Hannah told her. "And you're going to stay exactly where you are until your father is behind the wheel of the RV and ready to leave."

Everyone in the room laughed, including Nancy.

Nancy knew there was no use trying to fight Hannah when she had made up her mind about something. She looked over at her father. "Have you finished the paperwork, Dad?"

"Indeed I have, Nancy," Carson Drew replied. "Hannah's signed it already, and now, then, Jimmy, if you'd just sign here and give me one dollar, the farm and all its contents are yours."

Jimmy picked up a pen and signed where Mr. Drew pointed.

"It's done," Carson Drew said. "This copy is yours, and I'll take care of the rest of it."

"I don't know how to thank you," Jimmy said.

"You don't have to thank me, Jimmy," Carson Drew said. "It was Nancy's idea to ask Derek's mother to look for the missing letters. They were in a drawer in his bedroom. I picked them up this morning."

"I'm so glad we found those letters," Hannah said. "I would have felt terrible if I had sold this house when Bertha wanted you to have it all along." She sniffed. "When I read those letters, I could tell that Bertha had come to think of you as the son she never had."

"I felt like she was the mother I thought I had lost, too," Jimmy said. "But don't you need the money you would have made from the sale of the house?"

Hannah shook her head. "I already have a wonderful home with the Drews, Jimmy." She gave Nancy and Mr. Drew a big smile. "I don't need anything else."

Jimmy put his arms around Mary. "Now we can get married," he said.

Outside, a bolt of lightning struck a tree, splitting it in two. Distant thunder rumbled, shaking the house.

"We're in another tornado watch," Jimmy said. "The weather bureau expects really severe weather tonight."

"Then we should start for River Heights right away," Carson Drew said.

"That's a good idea, Dad," Nancy said. She slowly got out of bed. "Jimmy, I wish you and Mary the best of luck, and I hope you have a wonderful life together," she said, "but I just can't deal with another tornado."

"You know, this really doesn't happen all the time," Jimmy said, "but there are a few weeks every spring when you begin to think it does."

Nancy nodded. "Unfortunately, that's the time we picked to visit Medicine Bluff."

Mr. Drew handed Jimmy the keys to the farmhouse. "Here you are, Jimmy and Mary. Welcome home." He turned to Nancy. "Well, if everyone's ready, I guess we'd better start back to River Heights."

Through the bedroom window, Nancy saw a dark cloud that seemed to have a circular motion in it.

"Ready when you are, Dad," Nancy said. "I've flown in a tornado once, and I'd rather make the trip back in an RV any day."

Do your younger brothers and sisters want to read books like yours?

Let them know there are books just for *them!*

They can join Nancy Drew and her best friends as they collect clues and solve mysteries in

T H E

N A N C Y   D R E W

N O T E B O O K S ®

Starting with

#1 The Slumber Party Secret

#2 The Lost Locket

#3 The Secret Santa

#4 Bad Day for Ballet

AND

Meet up with suspense and mystery
in The Hardy Boys® are: The Clues Brothers™

Starting with

#1 The Gross Ghost Mystery

#2 The Karate Clue

#3 First Day, Worst Day

#4 Jump Shot Detectives

 A MINSTREL® BOOK

Published by Pocket Books

The most puzzling mysteries...
The cleverest crimes...
The most dynamic
brother detectives!

The
Hardy Boys®

By Franklin W. Dixon

Join Frank and Joe Hardy in up-to-date
adventures packed with action and suspense

Look for brand-new mysteries
wherever books are sold

Available from Minstrel® Books
Published by Pocket Books

**The Fascinating Story of
One of the World's Most
Celebrated Naturalists**

Celebrating
40 years
with the
wild
chimpanzees

MY LIFE *with the* CHIMPANZEES

by **JANE GOODALL**

From the time she was girl, Jane Goodall dreamed
of a life spent working with animals. Finally, when she
was twenty-six years old, she ventured into the forests
of Africa to observe chimpanzees in the wild. On her
expeditions she braved the dangers of the jungle
and survived encounters with leopards and lions
in the African bush. And she got to know an amazing
group of wild chimpanzees—intelligent animals whose
lives bear a surprising resemblance to our own.

Illustrated with photographs

A Byron Preiss Visual Publications, Inc. Book

A Minstrel® Book
Published by Pocket Books

2403

American S·I·S·T·E·R·S

Join different sets of sisters
as they embark on the varied,
sometimes dangerous,
always exciting journeys
across America's landscape!

West Along the Wagon Road, 1852

A *Titanic* Journey Across the Sea, 1912

Voyage to a Free Land, 1630

Adventure on the Wilderness Road, 1775

Crossing the Colorado Rockies, 1864

By Laurie Lawlor

A MINSTREL® BOOK

Published by Pocket Books

2200